When Eagles Fall

Mary Casanova

HYPERION BOOKS FOR CHILDREN
NEW YORK

For all who suffer loss
and find the strength to carry on

With special thanks for the generosity of eagle researcher
Dr. Bill Bowerman; Voyageur National Park biologist Lee Grim;
and The Raptor Center biologist Matt Solensky,
who hear the cry of eagles

First Edition
1 3 5 7 9 10 8 6 4 2
Printed in the United States of America
Library of Congress Cataloging-in-Publication Data on file
ISBN 0-7868-0665-6 (hc)   ISBN 0-7868-2557-X (lib)

Visit www.hyperionchildrensbooks.com

Also by Mary Casanova

Curse of a Winter Moon
Stealing Thunder
Wolf Shadows
Riot
Moose Tracks

Contents

The day is done, and the darkness
Falls from the wings of Night,
As a feather is wafted downward
From an eagle in his flight.

From "The Day Is Done"
Henry Wadsworth Longfellow

CHAPTER ONE

Captive

The orange bag descended, branch by branch, from the eagle's nest. Alex waited below with two other team members. She craned her neck, fingers laced under the sweaty knot of her bandanna and stubby ponytail. This was their ninth nest of the day, and, shoulders to neck, her muscles pinched and burned.

Above the white pine, two bald eagles circled, protesting. Alex had heard the piercing *kri-kri, kri-kri* of adult eagles before, but the cry they made when an eaglet was ripped from its nest was different. Somewhere between a pig's grunt and her mom's tongue-click scolding.

"Got it," Ned called. Like the Green Giant, fully

uniformed in Park Service green, he carried the wriggling bag to a patch of ground Alex had cleared of sticks and twigs. His wife, Maya, was busy arranging supplies at the edge of the banding site.

With a handheld scale, Ned weighed the bird, then slid the orange fabric down around its body. Dark brown feathers and black, intelligent eyes appeared. Beak open, the eaglet's pinkish-white tongue fluttered wildly. The eaglet was no doubt bewildered by what was happening.

And little wonder. It was a captive, just like her. If Alex hadn't landed herself in the emergency room, she'd still be back in San Jose, where she belonged. But Mom had overreacted, panicked, and phoned Alex's dad—something she avoided at all costs since their separation—and told him, "I'm worried, Russ. I really think Alex needs a change of friends and scenery for a while."

A deerfly landed on Ned's glistening bald head, but he ignored it. In one smooth motion, Ned flipped the eaglet on its back and put his green cap over the bird's head, quieting it. "Okay, Alex," he whispered. "You know what to do—you're getting to be a pro."

"Yeah, tell my dad that," she said quietly.

A tremble threaded through her chest. Her palms turned damp. She knelt in front of the eaglet, then carefully slid her hands, just as her dad had earlier shown her, along the eaglet's upper legs to its waxy, yellow ankles, just far enough down to keep the eaglet from flexing its talons and thrashing her bare knees. Its legs—just as surprising to her now as the first time—were *warm*. Poor bird didn't know what was going on.

"Abduction," she said, her voice rising. "Safe in its nest, then my dad snatches it. It's not really fair to the—"

"Hey, Alexis," her dad called from above. "Quiet, down there."

Alex felt like a scolded dog. She shot an angry glance at the camouflaged figure, eighty feet up, straddling the edge of the nest. "Hey, little fella," her father cooed to the remaining eaglet, "it's okay. I didn't mean to scare you."

She dropped her voice to a whisper. "Why is *he* the only one who can talk? It's like he thinks he's God or something."

Maya swatted deerflies circling above her black hair, which fell in a braid to the top of her sweatpants. In her eyes, strong and dark as coffee, a smile played, and she whispered, "Alex, when it comes to eagle research, Russell *is* God."

"He likes things quiet for the birds," Ned added with a wink, "but sometimes he breaks his own rules."

Alex huffed. "That's for sure." She knew her father was a respected eagle expert who had authored three books and read his research papers around the globe, that he had even studied the huge Steller's sea eagles in eastern Russia.

She knew better than anyone how he could talk for hours about what he loved most—eagles. That wasn't the point. Actually, she wasn't sure what the point was anymore. But Maya and Ned were her parents' old friends from Minnesota, where she used to live when she was younger. Her father's old friends. Why did she think they'd understand?

She held the eaglet's legs firmly, but not white knuckled as she had at the start of the day. Still, she knew she was hardly a pro. If her dad paid more attention, though, he might notice that she'd caught on pretty quickly.

That morning at Grandma's Pantry, shoveling in the last of his platter-size blueberry pancake, her dad had said, "If your head's in the clouds today, Alexis, you're gonna get hurt. Understand?" Did he think she was stupid? She was thirteen, a teenager for over two months already. At his words, she'd looked away to a sign above the cook's serving window that read: THIS AIN'T BURGER KING. YOU GET IT MY WAY, OR YOU DON'T GET IT AT ALL. Sounded just like her dad.

Working quickly, Ned and Maya Naatuck plucked three feathers from the bird's chest, drew blood from an artery beneath its wing, filled a tube and smeared blood on glass and paper, then sealed samples in envelopes.

While they worked, a mosquito lighted on Alex's thigh, dropped its needle nose, and began pumping up. She tried to ignore it. Her legs were already covered with red scratches like lines on a city street map; welted from mosquitoes, horseflies, and deerflies; and sore from squatting beside eaglets all day. She should have worn jeans as her dad had suggested, but she'd never admit that now.

"Last," Ned said, "ID tags." Using the rivet gun, he clamped a blue metal band on one of the eaglet's legs and a silver on the other. Then he spun the bands. "Gotta make sure they're loose," he said. "Still got some growin' to do, but she's good sized, for six weeks."

"Why does my dad call all the eaglets 'fellas'?" As soon as she'd asked, Alex wished she hadn't. Her mouth turned chalky. She knew the answer without having to ask. She could never be the boy her father once carried on his shoulders when they all went star catching. "Catch a falling star," her father sang, "and put it in a socket, Make your brown hair turn gray. . . ."

"Who knows anything, really," Maya said, "about how your dad thinks."

With a sharp breath, Alex forced her feelings down.

"Are you okay?" Maya whispered, the words merely forming on her lips.

Alex swallowed around a knot, nodded, and focused on the eaglet lying helpless before her. Concentrate on your grip, she commanded herself. Hold on. Stay in control.

Ned pulled his cap off the eaglet's head, and the bird startled. "Okay, back to your nest," he said, and eased the bag down over the eaglet's head and chest. "Now," he said, and Alex released her grip—at just the right second—and the nylon fabric slipped over the outstretched talons. "Perfect," Ned said, "that was just perfect." As he lifted the bag, the eaglet wriggled inside, righting itself before its return to the nest.

Stiff from squatting, Alex stood and stretched. As she did, the edge of her tank top tickled her new belly ring. When her dad climbed down, she'd stretch again to show it off, just to make him mad.

Through the bag's cinched opening, Alex caught a glance. Head cocked, the eaglet looked back with one bright, intelligent, steady eye. Watching her.

The runabout skimmed across Rainy Lake, and Alex faced backward, determined to not speak a word to her father, who sat across from her. The Evinrude motor churned a foamy white wake. In the distance, lake blended into sky without any line of green to separate the two. She could almost imagine that it was the Pacific, and that she wasn't so far away from home.

Stepping off the puddle-jumping plane in northern Minnesota was like arriving on another planet. The "Icebox of the Nation," International Falls was a paper-mill town that boasted the world's largest thermometer in the park beside its downtown, a whole three city blocks long. The city was like Alcatraz—remote and isolated—sitting on the edge of endless woods and water. There was no escaping, no running away.

"Banished," she said angrily. And that was exactly the right word for it.

"What'd you say?" her father asked.

"Nothing," she said, with enough sharpness to make him think twice about talking to her.

The hum of the boat motor filled the air between them. From the corner of her eye, she checked out her dad. He wore his brown cap backward, a middle-aged guy trying to look like a teenager. His plaid shirt stretched thin at his shoulders, and at his elbow a flap of ripped fabric hung in a V. Sweat and dirt layered his face, creased darkly into the crinkles along his eyes and the edges of his dry lips. The dirtier he was, the harder the day, the more trees he'd climbed, the happier he seemed. She looked away, wished she could disappear into that invisible line between water and air.

The boat sped on and passed a nest on a small island. "See that nest on Skipper Rock Island?" Her father pointed. "Two eaglets in that one."

Caught in amber light, the nesting tree leaned into the island's western edge. She wasn't blind. The nest was like an upside-down beaver lodge, right on top. You couldn't miss it. Unlike most of the mammoth pines her father climbed, the tree was short and skinny. You wouldn't need spikes and straps and climbing ropes. Not far from the nest, like a sentry keeping watch, a bald eagle perched on a dead tree stump.

"When Ned and I did our flyby last week to check the nests, something glinted from that one. Another blasted lure, no doubt."

Alex didn't say anything. She pretended she didn't care. At the base of other trees they'd found skeletons of northern pike and suckers, feathers from seagulls and crows, a squirrel's tail, fishing line, a battered teddy bear, and a half-dozen lures. When eagles brought fish back to the nest, fishing lures that had been snagged on a fish's body or mouth came with the eagle's catch.

Skipper Rock Island shrank steadily in the boat's wake, one of a thousand islands in the winding wilderness lake. The nest was one of many nests. Still, something about the nest tugged at Alex. Two eaglets that had bumped into each other since birth, probably fought over food together, tucked snugly in their feather-lined nest. One wrong move, and a lure might snag them. A curious peck could mean death.

"Will you get the lure out tomorrow?" Her words slipped out.

"Tree's got a zipper down its side—struck by lightning. Climb it, and you're asking for trouble."

"But what about the eaglets? You're the expert." Her voice was rude, but she couldn't seem to talk with her father anymore without a bite in her tone. She pressed ahead. "Someone has to help them."

His chest rose and fell with a deep breath. "The tree's

weak and might not hold my weight. It's a risk for the climber and the nest, too. Let's hope the parents do some housecleaning."

"I don't weigh much. I could—"

"Alexis, " he said, crossing his arms, glancing at her with a tilt of his head. "No. Don't even think about it."

She was lighter, smaller, parakeet-bone skinny. She suddenly remembered. *Parakweet.* That's what her brother had called her after her first-grade skit, when she'd dyed her hair blue to match her blue papier-mâché wings. How old had he been then? Three? Four? She wondered if her father remembered the nickname. It had been a long time since she'd heard it.

The nest faded to an ashen smudge on the edge of the island. In her mind, she could see the two eaglets. She couldn't stop thinking about them. If her dad—*God*—wasn't able to help the eaglets, maybe she could.

CHAPTER TWO

Naatuck's Cabin

The boat nudged toward the wooden dock. Heavy with exhaustion, Alex grabbed her backpack and piled out of the boat after the others. The moment her feet hit shore, mosquitoes began to circle.

"I'll get the sauna goin'," said Maya.

"And I'll get the drinks flowin'," Ned chimed in after her.

Alex's dad cleared his throat and shot Ned a look.

Ned apologized, palms outstretched. "Hey, not that we're big drinkers here. A couple beers, that's all I mean. And pop for those who are underage, of course."

Alex pretended not to hear. She didn't like to think

about how much Maya and Ned might know. Head down, she passed the sand beach and overturned green canoe, the pansy-filled rock garden and fire pit. Maya, whose arms were already filled with birch logs, was heading to the sauna building. "Taking a sauna?" she asked.

Alex shook her head and climbed the wooden steps to the Naatucks' cabin, a log home that Maya and Ned lived in all year. In the summer they boated to their island, and in the winter they drove their truck across the lake, except for freeze up and spring thaw, when the ice was too weak; then they stayed in town at an apartment.

The screen door creaked as Alex entered, amazed that the Naatucks didn't lock up when they left for the day. A pair of snowshoes hung crisscrossed above the stone fireplace. Butterball, their overweight tiger-striped cat, uncurled herself in an overstuffed chair, arched her back, then lay down again.

"Another ambitious day?" Alex asked. Pausing to scratch the cat between its ears, she crossed the braided rug to the porch, her room for the next week. Not fancy, but at least she had a place of her own. The faded couch waited for her like open arms. She flopped herself on top of her sleeping bag, and before she knew it, she was out.

Sometime in the dark of night, she woke with a start. At first she didn't know where she was. Her own bedroom . . . but she wasn't on her water bed. Her *abuela*

Elena's in Pismo Beach . . . but the air was wrong, sharp and piney, not seaside scented. Light flickered in the distance. Voices. Blinking, she sat up and rubbed her chilled arms. A mosquito buzzed. Minnesota. The light was a fire—a bonfire by the lake. The three silhouettes were familiar—the Naatucks and her father—sitting beside the fire on logs.

Voices floated up from shore, as if they were speaking through the screen, right next to her. Alex flopped down, climbed inside her flannel-lined sleeping bag, and closed her eyes.

"She was just acting out," Ned was saying. "All teens do."

"Well, getting into that kind of trouble"—her father's voice rose, uncertain, tinted with anger—"was a little more than acting out, in my mind. It's not like she's the first kid to go through a separation. I mean, not all teens end up in the emergency room."

A silence followed.

Alex lifted her hands to her ears, but midway she stopped herself and kept listening.

"Sometimes," her father continued, "I think she needs to live in a small town. Maybe I should talk her mother into sending her here to live with you two!" He laughed. "Hey, I give up. I mean, I try, but she shuts me out the minute I say *anything*. I send her gifts. You think I ever get a thank-you in return?"

"Shhh," Maya said. "Not so loud. Listen, you can't give up on her, Russ. She—"

"Sometimes," her father cut in, "I honestly think we do better when we're thousands of miles apart."

A loon's song drifted up from the lake, filling the air like the saddest song played on a violin. Alex let the haunting sound float over her, through her. If she still had her violin, she'd try composing a loon song, something that matched this northern bird's melancholy cry. The first night she'd heard it, it made her shiver. Now she swallowed back feelings of aching sadness. She couldn't remember ever feeling so lonely.

"Maybe this week is just what the two of you need," Ned said.

"I admit—I had hopes that we'd get along, but looks like we're off to a pretty shaky start." There was a pause. "Okay, okay. End of subject. Here's to two successful days of banding eagles on beautiful Rainy Lake. As they say in Sweden, *skol!*"

"*Nastrovia!*" Ned said. "As they say in Russia."

"How about a good old-fashioned 'cheers!'?" Maya added.

A clinking of glass followed.

Alex wriggled deeper into her sleeping bag until it covered her head. When her father had been in Sweden the year before, at least he had acted happy to talk with her on the phone. Maybe his enthusiasm was just that he loved being halfway around the world, as far away from her as possible. He'd sent her a small carved horse, hand painted red, that she kept on her windowsill. Now she wished she could pick it up and throw it.

When she finally slept, she dreamed of tubes in her arms, tubes down her throat, tubes attached to a hundred IVs around her hospital bed. Red horses trampled her violin, the violin she'd sold at the pawnshop a city bus ride away from her house. An eaglet was falling from its nest, and in her dream, she became the eaglet . . . falling . . . falling . . . falling. . . .

Gray light surrounded her when she awoke.

Her father was at her side, a tall shadow. "Alexis? Alexis?"

She tried to open her eyes wider, but they shut again. "Alex," she mumbled. "My friends call me Alex."

"Time to get up," he said. "We're heading out soon. Breakfast at Grandma's Pantry, remember?"

She moaned and pulled the edge of the sleeping bag over her head. His feet shifted on the wooden floorboards.

"Want to take the day off?"

"Mm-hmm," she answered, and instantly fell back to sleep.

By the time she stirred again, sun flickered on aspen leaves and fell in golden prisms across the porch. Outside the screen, a brown sparrow sat on a cedar branch, warbling, as if to say, "Finally get up-up-up-up-up!"

Alex slipped into her leather sandals, stepped out the porch door, and trudged along the path behind the cabin. Knee-high ferns tickled her legs as she headed to the outhouse. The Naatucks had apologized that they hadn't switched their log cabin over to civilized living yet with a fully plumbed bathroom, but they promised one was coming before the year 3000. An outhouse. "You expect me to use that?" she'd said to her father. "Sure," he'd answered, as if it were no big deal. Maybe she had overreacted. This morning, the outhouse with its carved crescent moon looked plush compared to squatting in the woods again. She held her breath and headed in, trying not to study its dark corners for spiders, then made her way back outside again, gulping fresh air.

Below, the lake was dappled with silver coins of sunlight. The runabout was gone. She'd never heard the Naatucks and her father leave. An unexpected pang filled her. She hadn't been alone—completely alone—since she could remember. A hollow, tickling sensation filled her. She almost wished she had gone with them. Yet all she'd wanted since she'd arrived was to be left alone. She couldn't figure out what she wanted anymore.

Just beyond the canoe, a mallard and half a dozen ducklings scuttled in the bay, dipping up and down, tiny tails pointing skyward. The mother kept her head high, alert for danger.

The eaglets on Skipper Rock were in danger, and their

parents probably didn't have a clue. They might be keeping watch for a hungry bear that could scale their nesting tree or working hard to find enough food for their young, but the lure in their nest was an immediate threat. Perhaps the bald eagles would do some housecleaning as her dad had said, but what if they didn't?

The island couldn't be far, a few minutes' paddle, at most. She eyed the canoe. If she left now, she could be back before long. When her dad returned, she'd hold out the lure and he'd say, "Hey, where'd you get that?"

"The eagles' nest," she'd reply. Not haughtily, just matter-of-factly. He liked matter-of-fact best. Keep the emotion out of it, that's what he always said. "Somebody had to do it," she'd say. "I couldn't just let those eaglets live in peril." She smiled to herself and glanced at the fire pit.

No smoldering ashes, no scattered beer bottles. She remembered the night before, how her father had talked about her behind her back, probably told Maya and Ned everything. More than they needed to know. Now they'd look at her differently, as if she belonged in a juvenile detention home, certainly not at their cabin. Most definitely not to stay with them permanently, as her father had joked. Real funny. Maybe she'd toss the lure at his feet instead. "There," she'd say, arms crossed, "if you really cared about eagles, you would have gotten the lure out of the nest!"

She headed to the boat shed. Dank and dark, it was

filled with boat motors, gas cans, and tools. In one corner stood a branch with an abandoned hornets' nest, and to her left hung fishing rods and life jackets. Alex pulled a blue-and-yellow life jacket off a peg and zipped it over her tank top; then she grabbed a wooden paddle.

She could do this. Maybe her dad thought she had her head in the clouds, but she'd prove him wrong. How hard could it be to paddle a canoe or climb a tree? Part of her didn't even know why helping the eaglets had suddenly become so important, so deep-down urgent. But it had. She knew—more clearly than she'd known anything in a long, long time—she had to try.

CHAPTER THREE

On a Mission

Alex dropped the paddle on the sandy beach, ran to the cabin, packed herself a lunch, refilled her water bottle, and grabbed her long-sleeved cotton shirt, jeans, a windbreaker, and a box of Band-Aids—just in case. She rummaged through the kitchen cupboards, ate a bowl of Cheerios, and downed a glass of tangerine-orange juice. Then, backpack over her shoulder, she ran down the steps before she changed her mind.

One thing was certain. She had to get to Skipper Rock Island before her father returned, and she wasn't sure how long he'd be gone or how many nests he was going to climb on the last day of banding. If he saw her climbing the nest, he'd be more than a little angry. After all, *he* had permits to climb; she didn't. But if someone else asked what she was doing, she'd just say, "I'm with the eagle-banding project with Dr. Russell Reed, from the U of M." She'd sound official enough to keep anybody from stopping her.

Buoyed by a sense of mission, she pushed the canoe into the lake, climbed over the bow, and settled into the stern seat. The canoe wobbled and threatened to tip. How in the world was a person supposed to get anywhere in one of these? Finally she settled herself, lifted the paddle, and started off.

At first, the canoe swerved wildly, a sidewinder snake, S-ing its way across water. Gradually she learned to dip the paddle straight alongside the canoe, not in a wide arc, and the canoe moved ahead more easily. She paddled left, then right, water dripping down the length of the wooden paddle onto her bare thighs and sandaled feet. But that was okay. The water was cool, the air was warm, even though the billowy clouds were piling up, threatening to cover up the sun.

A breeze skittered over the bay. Just beyond the point, a loon popped up, a sprinkling of white confetti across its black back. It studied her with its red eye. Alex waited for the loon to sing, but it was silent. In an arcing motion, it dove. For a few moments, Alex waited, watching for it to surface. She had nearly given up when it popped up beyond the point to the east. In the direction of the nest. *A sign.*

She laughed to herself. If her mom sold a blue house, it meant God was giving her a sign to buy that new midnight-blue Volkswagen Bug. If her mother came down with a sore throat and fever, it was a sign that God was trying to teach her something: *slow down*. Alex liked to tease her. They'd been standing at a stoplight in San Jose and she'd said, "Hey, Mom, it's green. Must be a sign that we should cross, huh?"

That time her mom had been pretty quick. She stood, silver hoops in her ears, dark hair falling to her shoulders, and silk shirt shimmering in the sun, and pointed as the light changed to red. "See that?"

"Yeah?"

"Well, that's a sign that you should stop being so sarcastic."

Alex had only meant it as a joke, and her mom had taken it the wrong way. But lately, barbed words seemed to slip regularly from her tongue. *Sarcastic*. That was probably the word for it. For a time, she'd worked really hard at being her parents' "dream child." The more they fought, the harder she had tried to be good, to fill the growing gap between them. She maintained straight A's, barely taking time to see her best friend, Mercedes, after school or on weekends; kept her bedroom spotless, with everything on a shelf or in a drawer, not stuffed under the bed or strewn across the floor; set her alarm extra early so she wouldn't be late in the morning. For a while, she'd nearly killed herself trying. She should be first chair in South Penning's junior-high orchestra. But the day Sky-Li approached Alex at her locker, everything changed. Sky-Li had asked with her sweet, high-pitched voice, "So, do you ever have any time to have fun?" That was the same day Alex's parents announced at dinner that they were separating. That evening Alex decided that if they could quit, then so could she.

With each dip of the paddle, Alex felt better, the tightness in her chest easing. She breathed the crisp air. No hint of gas fumes, only the smell of cedar, pine, lake water, and yesterday's bug spray. She followed the shoreline, leaving behind people—civilization. The Naatucks' was the last cabin on the main island; to the east it was miles of water and national park.

Along the shore, a fallen pine tree stretched out into the lake, limbless and bare. Upon it, a line of sharp-headed ducks—mergansers—rested in a row. As the canoe neared, the brown birds dropped into the water, dove and surfaced, then scuttled away from the canoe.

Dip, stroke, dip, stroke. Change sides. Dip, stroke, dip, stroke. Change sides. She developed a pattern. Now she understood why voyageurs sang when they paddled; it helped them keep a rhythm. The first place her father had taken her when she arrived was to the park's visitor's center, as if it were a beacon of teaching that could guide her in ways he could not. She had groaned and plopped down in the minitheater on a padded chair and watched the slide show. French music of the voyageurs. A narrator hyping up the Park's natural beauties. The nation's only water-access national park. Endless pristine wilderness. Hype, hype, hype, hype. Slides of the park in all seasons. She'd laughed out loud at the tent in the snow. Really, you'd have to be insane to think camping in the winter in below-freezing temps was a good time. What was the word they'd used in the slide show? *Exhilarating*, that was it. Well, the most exhilarating thing she could think of would be to get back on the plane in three days and fly home. Home to her new friends. Home to her life.

She paddled on, lifted along by a breeze at her stern. At least she knew a few nautical words: *stern, bow, starboard, port*. In the past months, her mom had been seeing a guy named Oscar Inness, who owned a sailboat at the marina near Abuela Elena's apartment. Mom had been throwing boating words around in the past few months as if she were the first mate.

"Mom," Alex had asked. "Why would someone name their boat something as geeky as *Dream Wings*?"

"What's wrong with that?" Her mom tipped her brass watering can into the potted orange tree in the living room. "I think that it's a . . . well, a hopeful name." Then she spoke to the plant. "I'm sorry I let you get bone-dry. You must be thirsty." She stood up and smoothed her floral silk skirt, her eyes brighter than Alex had seen them in a long time. For months, ashen semimoons had rested permanently beneath her mom's eyes; anything could set her crying. "Honey," she said. "Oscar's really very kind—a sweet man. I hope you'll get a chance to meet him soon. And who knows, you might even like him."

Alex huffed. "Don't hold your breath. I mean, how long did you say he's owned the sailboat and hasn't taken it out of the harbor yet?"

Her mom paused and refastened her ponytail. "Two years," she finally answered.

"See? My point exactly. I mean, where's the guy's sense of adventure and all that?"

"Alex." Her mom was firm. "He's not your father."

"That's not what I—" Alex stopped short. She hadn't meant to point to her dad. She felt herself bristle like a cornered dog. Some topics were better left alone.

"Alex, I know that my seeing someone else isn't easy for—"

"Oh, whatever," Alex said sourly. "I don't care anymore. It's your life." She let the screen door slam behind her.

That Saturday morning, Alex had padded from her bed to the kitchen, looking forward to her mom's traditional school's-out breakfast of sausage, omelettes, granola-cranberry muffins, and fresh-squeezed orange juice. The breakfast had been a tradition since kindergarten. But then she remembered. Her mom had chosen instead to leave early that morning for Pismo Beach. For Oscar Inness. The note read: *Help yourself to frozen waffles and pizza. Have fun at the Mertonsons'. Be back tomorrow night. Love, Mom.* And a phone number.

Alex had begged to stay at Janelle's, but her mom hadn't approved, because she didn't know Alex's new friends. So instead she'd arranged for Alex to stay with a couple who had no kids of their own, two realtors who worked with Alex's mom. That morning, feeling angry—and wandering around in a house that echoed like a conch shell—she decided to make her own plans. Janelle was having a party. And Alex was going.

She rested the paddle across her lap, and let the wind blow her toward the farthest point of Dryweed Island. Other islands dotted the south shore, and a steady stream of boats followed a charted course: red buoys on your right, green on your left, at least when you were heading in one direction. Mostly the boats followed the channels. Outside the channels, you'd have to follow a nautical map; rocks hid dangerously beneath the lake's surface. At least with a canoe, you couldn't destroy your motor, or as Ned put it, "take out your lower unit."

The canoe turned sideways to the wind and began to rock heavily, back and forth. Alex carved the paddle through the waves and turned the bow downwind. The last thing she needed was to tip over before she even got to Skipper Rock Island. Her biceps began to ache, and she was certain a rock had lodged itself between her shoulder blades.

The sun had rounded its midpoint in the sky and was moving to the west. At the rate the canoe was going, Alex would get there just as fast if she swam to the island. But now the waves were building, pushing her more quickly toward the islands beyond Dryweed.

Alex kept paddling, trying to ignore the hot pain she felt in her arms. If she paddled every day, she'd grow stronger and her arms wouldn't hurt so much. She knew that. It was the same principle as going out for the swim team. The first day in the chlorine left her arms like putty, but within two weeks, she'd built muscle and could swim farther and faster than she'd thought possible. She might have been good if she hadn't quit at the end of week number three.

Then she spotted a flash of white. At the western edge of Skipper Rock, on the same dead tree stump, a bald eagle was keeping watch. With eyesight six times stronger than a human's, the eagle was certainly watching her every move.

The eagle lifted from its perch and swooped down across her path, its talons tucked beneath its massive body, its beak yellowish-gold. Alex flinched. Was she going to climb the tree—really? And if the eagle decided to defend the nest? Her father had climbed countless times and never once been attacked—even though he said an eagle in

Montana had raked one climber's shoulders. Alex was probably safe from the adults. It was the eaglets she was afraid of. They weren't as predictable.

She cleared the distance from Dryweed to Skipper Rock. Beyond the shelter of the large island, wind whistled in her ears and pushed the canoe forward. If the wind kept up, would her father return early? She'd have to hurry. She stopped paddling and studied the nest.

Ahead in the treetop, a clump of branches jutted against the graying sky. Her eagles' nest. She had it planned. She'd head to the sheltered side of the island, out of the wind, and pull the canoe up onshore. Like her father, she'd be decisive, quick, and levelheaded. And she wouldn't talk. If it was better for the birds to have no talking, then she wouldn't say a word. She wouldn't be like her dad, who made rules and then broke them.

As she cleared the edge of the island, the wind grabbed the canoe and pulled it off course. Alex leaned forward, straining her back muscles, and reached deeper into the water with the paddle, doubling her pace, to stay close to the island's shore. The lake beyond, as she'd learned from the slide show, stretched eighty miles from end to end. She didn't want to think about being blown *that* far off course.

She aimed toward the brown Park Service sign planted on the sheltered shore. ISLAND SITE CLOSED, the sign read. NESTING EAGLES. DO NOT DISTURB.

Alex paused. She would be breaking the rules, but she

needed to help the eaglets. And her father had refused to remove the lure. He gave her no other choice. She dipped the paddle, pulled hard, and floated closer.

Heart quickening, she looked up. A bald eagle circled, wings flat against the sky, crying its alarm.

CHAPTER FOUR

The Climb

A boat motor hummed somewhere behind her.

"Oh no," Alex groaned, certain her father had spotted her. She turned her head as the canoe bumped rocks, jolting her from her seat, and fell onto her knees on the floor of the canoe.

"Hey!" called a guy from behind her. "Don't bother the eagles!"

"What're you doin'?" a girl added. "That's a protected island!"

Rattled, Alex sat back on the seat.

The voices came from a sparkling red speedboat filled with a half dozen teenagers. Three girls in the bow, three guys in the seats. A blonde in a lavender two-piece stood up and pointed to the sign. "Didn't you see the sign?"

"Uh . . . sorry, missed it!" Alex called lamely, back paddling from shore. She kept paddling, increasing the distance between herself and the island, and then, when the speedboat roared away, she drifted, letting the waves rock her back and forth. She hated being scolded by teenagers not much older than herself. Part of her wished she could join them. Maybe they were friendly, people she could hang out with. Anything would be better than returning to spend time with the Naatucks and her father, who talked about her behind her back.

Now two eagles circled the island. It wasn't that eagles wouldn't nest when people were nearby, Ned had explained, but the sign helped to keep people from staying too close for too long. If boaters and campers stayed on the island, the adult eagles would circle endlessly, leaving the eaglets exposed to hunger and bad weather. As Alex saw it, she would disturb the nest for only a short time. In the end, she might be saving one of the eaglets' lives.

Alex could understand how parents could neglect their young if disturbed by outside forces. Hadn't it happened with her own parents? They'd spent so much energy, every ounce of it, trying to protect her brother. Like the eagles, they'd circled and cried, worried and fretted, not seeing that their actions to fend off his sickness were in some ways making things worse. They fought more and more with each other. During a particularly bad fight, her dad threw a carton of eggs on the floor; her mom swore and screamed, "You're heartless!" They blamed each other and neglected to see they had another child: her.

A boat motor droned in the distance, growing fainter and fainter. She listened intently for approaching boats. Nothing. A breeze swooshed through the pine boughs towering above the island. Seagulls cried somewhere beyond her view. She paddled back and nudged the canoe to shore.

Backpack on her shoulders, she climbed over the canoe's yoke to the bow and heaved the canoe over the rocks, struggling with low cedar branches until it was hidden. The shiny green of the canoe, like the shell of a beetle, would be impossible to hide completely, but now it wouldn't be easy to spot from a distance.

She walked to a circular steel fire pit and campsite area, only yards from the nesting site. If the island weren't off-limits, maybe she'd return here with a tent and be by herself for a few days. Just her and the eagles. Of course, she knew she couldn't. The island would remain closed to visitors until the nesting season was over, sometime in August. Too much human activity wouldn't be good for the birds. Suddenly she almost felt like her father. She brushed the idea away. He was the last person she wanted to resemble. *God* was a bit too hard for a human like herself to live up to.

In a bed of grass, she dropped her backpack. She pulled out her baggy jeans and slipped them over her shorts. She threw her long-sleeved shirt—wrinkled, the way she liked it—over her tank top and knotted it just above her belly button. Then, on second thought, she untied the knot. She needed to save her skin from scrapes when she climbed.

She followed a skinny path toward the nesting tree. Light-green lichen crunched beneath her weight. Blueberry plants covered a slope, berries still tiny and white, a long way from ripening.

Near shore, immediately below the nest, eagle droppings covered leaves like white paint. Amid a pile of discarded sticks lay two fish skeletons, the tail of a squirrel, and several black feathers. Crows, most likely. At least she wasn't about to climb a turkey vulture's nest, she reminded herself. "Turkey vultures feed on anything dead," her father had explained, "and their nests are writhing with maggots." She squirmed inside, remembering.

She tilted her head and surveyed the climb. With the nest directly overhead, she couldn't see any sign of the eaglets. The parents circled in the graying sky. That meant the eaglets had to be there, hunkered down. Her skin prickled. She took a deep breath and studied her approach. If she panicked, she'd be useless. The lower limbs of the white pine were gone. How was she supposed to get up the tree if she couldn't get started?

A smaller pine tree ran parallel to the nesting tree, only

a foot away. The smaller tree would make a good step stool to the large pine. She found a limb for her foot, a limb for her hand, and began to climb. She touched something sticky and groaned. She'd forgotten about pitch, sappy and sticky and strongly pine scented. Her hands would be pasted with the stuff. She paused and examined her free hand, now flecked brownish-black with bark bits and pitch. "Ah—so what?" she whispered. Compared to the importance of removing the lure, what did getting a little dirty matter? When she got back, she'd hit the sauna for a good cleaning.

She kept going, hand up, then foot, then hand. Pausing, she glanced down. She was already ten feet up the smaller tree, and it had been easy. She could barely touch the big pine, yet knew she had to switch trees. Only a foot, maybe a foot and a half between the two trees, but the distance looked huge. A larger limb offered support, seemed to reach her way. She edged her foot over to it, slowly shifted her sticky hands from one set of branches to another. There.

On the nesting tree, she got her bearings. Looked down. Studied her way up, heart thumping. The nest shadowed her climb. It was a mass of sticks. How was she supposed to get over its edge? She drew a few deep breaths, then kept climbing, finding a knob of footing here, a solid branch there. Along the tree's length, a lightning strike had cut a line in the trunk from top to bottom, weakening it. But what could the added weight of a hundred-pound girl do to the tree? Surely it would hold. She hoped it would hold. Was she crazy for climbing the tree? Loco? She pictured the eaglets, the glint of a lure, and kept going.

Her neck began to ache from craning at the nest and its supporting branches directly above. How could her father climb to eight nests, sometimes a dozen, in a day? Sure, he used ropes and spikes, but the trees he climbed towered much higher than this one, their girth three or four times as wide.

Don't look down. If she looked down now, with thirty or forty feet between herself and the ground, she might stop. She might freeze. She kept her gaze forward. Upward. First one hand up, then one leg. Get around the next branch. Steady, steady. Up.

All too soon, she reached the base of the nest. She straddled a branch, pressed her forehead to the tree's trunk, and rested for a moment.

A slight rustle sounded above her.

"It's okay," she said softly, her voice wavering. "I'm not going to hurt you."

Maybe that's why her father talked. He couldn't help it. She hadn't planned to talk, but the words just came out.

She studied the fork where the nest was wedged. As her father had done with each nest, she'd have to clear debris from an edge so she could get a foothold. Squatting on the branch, with one hand around the tree, she reached to the nest and cleared away loose feathers and stuff she'd rather not think about—much of it falling into her hair and eyes.

Blinking back debris and dust, heart gathering speed, hoping, praying that it would hold, she grabbed the nest's strongest supporting branch, found the last knob on the tree's trunk, and, nearly breathless, pulled herself up—she *was* crazy!—and over the nest's edge.

She nearly fell headfirst into the nest, then steadied herself and sat back on her haunches. She was *in* an eagles' nest—a nest the size of a bathtub.

Two pairs of deep black eyes met her. Beaks wide, the eaglets hopped back, their talons almost as large as her own hands, which were shaking. At least she didn't have to worry about bagging the eaglets for research.

"I'd be scared, too," she cooed, "but don't worry. I won't hurt you." For a second, she glanced out. Whitecaps frosted the lake. Wind whistled through her hair. She was actually sitting on the edge of an eagles' nest. Her friends would never believe it. No wonder her father loved this work. Above, the sky was a soft gray, but to the west, thunderheads formed an ominous wall. Dread tied itself around her stomach. She'd better make her visit quick. She didn't need to become a lightning rod. Get the lure and go.

The nest was a downy-lined mass of sticks and twigs. A half-eaten fish lay in the center of the nest, nearly covering a silver lure. With one eye on the birds and one eye on the lure, Alex reached down. The lure's deadly barbs were half stuck in nest matter, and Alex wiggled the barbs free, pulling the jawbone of a fish with it.

In that moment, with that small motion, one of the eaglets flattened itself to the opposite side of the nest, wings slightly extended outward, its head turned sideways, watching her with one eye. But the other eaglet, the smaller of the two, scooted back, flapping its wings. *His* wings.

"Hey, little fella," she said, alarmed at the way the eaglet kept backing up. "Come on, now," she whispered, her throat suddenly dry. "Stay in your nest, little guy."

But the eaglet opened his dark beak wide, his tongue fluttering rapidly.

Overhead, a flash of white filled her vision. A pair of bald eagles circled, their raspy cries filling the air. "Don't worry," she said, hoping the adults would keep their distance as they usually did. One dive, one swipe from their talons, and—she put the idea out of her mind. She dropped the lure over the edge of the nest. "I'm leaving, I'm leaving."

Frantically the smaller eaglet began to flap his fledgling wings—half feathers, half fluffy down—and clawed awkwardly for footing on the nest's edge. He kept trying to back up, but there was nowhere to go. Then, as Alex watched in horror, the eaglet toppled backward, beyond her view, screeching once as he plummeted through tree branches toward the ground.

CHAPTER FIVE

The Eaglet

No matter how awful she felt, the only way down . . . was down. But she couldn't move. Couldn't budge her hands or her legs. She squatted in the nest and wanted to disappear, to rewind time, to wake up in the porch at the Naatucks' cabin, to find that what had just happened had been a terrible dream.

From the ground below rose a series of short, shrill cries. The eaglet was either dying or calling for help. Then the cries stopped altogether.

The distant wall of thunderheads, black as burned marshmallows, had drifted closer. The wind carried a scattering of raindrops. Overhead, the bald eagles continued to circle, endlessly circle, crying their raspy high-pitched alarm.

To the far side of the nest, the remaining eaglet pinned itself down, eye steadily watching. Accusing her.

Alex's mind whirred. If she ever made it down the tree again, how was she supposed to get the eaglet back in its nest? Her windbreaker. She'd wrap it up—somehow—and carry it up, avoiding its beak and talons, and get it back in its nest where it belonged. She'd managed to climb the tree. She'd done that, almost without thinking about what she was doing. She'd climbed it before she knew how scary it was. Could she climb it a second time with an eaglet? She wasn't at all sure.

A thin lightning streak zigzagged the dark horizon from sky to earth like the first line on an Etch A Sketch. She'd been good at that thing, twisting the knobs to create pictures. But her brother, his corkscrew sandy hair framing his brown eyes, had usually tried to mess up her efforts, just to irritate her. Crazy that he—Jonathan—should enter her mind now. She stared at the horizon, waiting for another shaft of light. Lightning. Then it dawned on her. It was as if her mind had been working in slow motion, not connecting the dots. She was in a treetop. A tree that had been struck once before. Why not again? It was a perfect lightning target.

Get down, she told herself. Move. You have to get down *now*. The tree was bending slightly with the wind.

Whitecaps frothed the lake in every direction. Some judge of weather she was. She should never have started out from shore.

Slowly Alex unclenched her hands from the nest, willing herself to let go. She swallowed hard, blinking past the sudden gush of tears to her eyes. Then she shifted her body around, away from the eaglet in the nest, and looked over the edge. The ground was incredibly far away. She couldn't do it. She'd just have to stay put until someone found her and carried her down or helicoptered her off the nest.

Her stomach lurched. Somehow she had to find her footing again over the edge of the nest, a tangle of sticks and feathers. What was to keep her from slipping and falling to the ground below? Probably serve her right.

The eaglet, she tried to assure herself, would be okay. Eagles were tough. She'd get down—first things first—and then figure out how to help the eaglet back to his nest. Heck, maybe he could fly. The thud sounded again in her memory. No. Not yet. At worst, she'd get help. She winced. And if she had to, she'd ask her father to help her get the eaglet back to his nest.

She edged closer to the limb that formed much of the nest's support. The limb she'd followed on her way up. Panic filled her. She couldn't do this.

Bass drums of thunder rolled in the distance.

Cautiously she moved her body back over her earlier path, back over the edge of the nest, legs dangling in the air. She kept moving until her waist buckled over the sharp sticks of the nest, scraping against a patch of bare skin, catching on her belly ring. She felt a sharp tug at her navel, but she wriggled slightly and came free. Still, she found no footing.

The wind picked up its tempo, and tree limbs creaked below her. She had to get down. Keeping her grip firm on the supporting limb, she kicked toward the underside of the nest, found a spot. Her foot caught and held. One of the spots she'd cleared out on her climb up. She eased her weight downward, sliding her hand along the limb, panicking at the open spaces around her, the dizzying feeling in her head. Maybe she'd just pass out and fall, and it would all be over before she felt anything.

She was closer now to the tree's crook. She eased herself lower, nearly losing her grip, but she held fast. There. Her foot hit the limb beneath the nest. She rested for a moment, both feet now on the limb, and glanced down. A flopping motion caught her eye. A few yards from the base of the tree, the eaglet—nearly camouflaged amid the brush and vegetation—flapped his wings. Flapped one wing.

No. Alex wanted to cry. Something was terribly wrong. Even from so high up, the eaglet shouldn't look so strange. As it flapped, one wing hung limp, oddly extended from his body. It must be broken.

39

She had to get to the eaglet.

She eyed her next move downward, gripped the nearest branch, and carefully climbed down. Foot first, then hand, then foot. Rest. Her limbs trembled. She licked her lips, suddenly dry. Take it one step at a time. She neared the base, her hands black and sticky, shifted over to the parallel tree, and dropped shakily to the ground.

The eaglet hopped away from her, his beak open wide.

"I won't hurt—" She stopped herself. Like a twig snapped nearly in half, his wing hung limp and touched the ground. "I can't tell you how sorry—" Alex blurted. "I didn't mean to hurt you, I didn't. I only wanted to help, to get the lure."

All actions are selfish, a voice in her head chided. Somewhere she'd heard that. That even when you think you're doing something out of the goodness of your heart, you're usually helping yourself somehow. She had meant to help the eaglets, hadn't she? Or was she helping herself, trying to make herself feel better somehow? It didn't matter now.

She glanced around the base of the tree for the lure. It had to be there, somewhere. It proved her intentions were good. She walked around the nesting tree and scanned the ground for a glint of silver. If she had to explain herself, the lure would prove why she'd come there. . . . She kept searching. She'd dropped it over the nest's edge. Finally she glanced up. Halfway up the tree, dangling from a thin branch, stopped by a whorl of pine needles, was the lure. At least it was no longer in the nest. The eaglets wouldn't peck at it now or get hooked by its barbs.

Alex let out a heavy sigh. She'd done a good thing, she was sure of it.

She turned back to the eaglet, now perched a foot off the ground on a mossy stump. His right wing hung crookedly at his side. He opened his beak wide, tongue fluttering wildly, turned his head, and watched her.

"I was trying to help," Alex said, tears in her voice. "Really I was."

Rain began to fall steadily, whipped along by the steady wind. Alex pushed wet strands of hair from her eyes, sat down a few yards from the eaglet, studying him and wondering what to do.

Water dripped off her nose and she shivered, arms clasped around her knees. She was getting soaked, even with the shelter of tree limbs above her. Rain ran in tiny rivulets off the eaglet's head. He shook his feathers. Usually, Alex remembered, adult eagles would spread their wings and protect their young from a storm. Now they were off their nest. If she didn't leave the island, neither of the eaglets would get the protection they needed from rain and wind.

The eaglet sat on the stump, eyeing her. He didn't seem afraid of her, or maybe he was in shock from his fall. She could leave the island and get help, but with predators—foxes, weasels, even bears—the eaglet would be vulnerable. She couldn't leave him alone. It might be hours before she could return with help. And the eaglet needed help. Her father's help. He'd know what to do with it. There were raptor centers, places where injured birds could be treated, where a broken wing might be mended. That's where this bird needed to go. She ran her forefinger over her bottom lip. And as much as she didn't want to confess what she'd done, she was going to have to bring the eaglet to her father.

She jumped up and ran along the path toward the campsite. Rain pelted her head and shoulders as she pulled her blue-and-teal windbreaker from her backpack. All she had to do was get it over the bird's head. All she had to do was get the eaglet into the canoe and back to the Naatucks' on Dryweed Island.

Maybe her dad thought she had her head in the clouds. And sometimes maybe she did, but she had to take charge now. She could do this, she knew she could.

When she reached the eaglet, he lay chest down in long grasses, right wing extended.

She crept closer, the hood of her windbreaker opened wide in her hands, ready. The bird didn't move.

In a swift motion, she dropped the hood of her windbreaker over the eaglet's head. The bird didn't move a feather. She grabbed the hood tassels and pulled them tight so that the hood cinched up around the eaglet's head.

For a second, the bird struggled, then quieted again.

Alex pushed wet bangs out of her eyes, then she crouched closer to the eaglet and—she could scarcely believe she was going to do this—grabbed the bird firmly and pulled him to her chest, his talons reaching outward, away from her.

The eaglet clawed the air with its yellow, waxy legs, its razor-sharp talons. But with his head encased by the hood of her jacket, he soon stopped struggling. He wasn't exactly heavy—maybe six pounds or so—but with every step toward the canoe, Alex's shoulders pinched from climbing, from paddling . . . from the weight of the eaglet's life in her hands.

CHAPTER SIX

Wind and Water

Rain dripped from cedar branches as Alex carried the eaglet to the canoe. The eaglet's heart fluttered against her own; his talons were flexed, sharp and ready. Ned had said that in just another week or two, the eaglets would be tough to handle. At this age they didn't realize how much power they really had. Alex was glad of that.

Gently Alex lowered herself to her knees beside the canoe and placed the eaglet chest down on the floor, just in front of the bow seat. Her hands stuck momentarily on the windbreaker, and the eaglet startled. He flapped beneath the fabric, stood on his feet, and lifted his covered head.

"C'mon, little guy, cooperate. Stay," she said, as if it were

Tooky, the yellow Lab her father had brought home for her when it was a puppy; the dog he couldn't care for because he traveled too much. He couldn't have a dog barking at the base of every eagles' nest. When her parents had split, Tooky went to live in Brainerd with Alex's grandparents. So much for the family dog.

Lifting the bow, Alex eased the canoe off the rock lip, scraping its underbelly as it dropped into the water. She kept glancing at the eaglet. Her paddle rested against a birch tree; she grabbed it and slid it into the canoe. Beyond the arms of the cove, waves hit jagged rocks and sprayed plumes of water skyward. Farther out, whitecaps, now a few feet high, frothed the lake. She could stay on the island and wait out the storm, but she wasn't very familiar with Minnesota weather. How long would a storm last? Minutes? Days? Her long-sleeved shirt and jeans were soaked. Wet to the bone, she'd rather be making progress, working her way back to the Naatucks' and some dry clothes. All she'd have to do was paddle, paddle hard, and she could make it. The distance between Skipper Rock and Dryweed was short. Once she reached Dryweed, she'd paddle close to shore, out of the wind. If she had to, she'd get out of the canoe and walk the shoreline back to the cabin.

The eaglet now lay motionless. What if he had broken more than his wing? He could have injured something inside when he fell. Carefully she stepped toward the canoe and slipped on wet moss—nearly falling headlong into the water—but landed instead on her rear. What a mess she was making of things.

Alex glanced up. Despite the rain, a bald eagle rode the wind currents, barely flapping its wings. She huddled into her shirt, imagining the parent's talons rake her neck as it watched her from above.

She hopped over the bow—really glad the eaglet's head was covered so he couldn't nip a chunk of flesh from her ankle—and managed not to tip the canoe as she made her way to the stern. She sat on the woven cane seat, gripped the paddle, and headed out of the sheltered bay, straight for the whitecaps.

She could do this. She wasn't like Oscar Inness, too afraid to try.

Yards out from the bay, water sprayed across the side of the canoe, hitting Alex full in the face, stinging her eyes. She blinked, trying to clear her vision. The canoe had turned sideways and water splashed over its edge.

"I need help!" Alex cried aloud, to the wind, to no one. Frantically she paddled hard on her right and gradually pointed the bow directly into the west wind. A wind that slammed into her like a semi, never braking, never letting up, just pushing her backward, away from Skipper Rock Island, even farther away from Dryweed.

For a moment, she held the canoe steady, bow windward, and the canoe rode up and down, riding onto one wave, then sloshing down into the valley of the next. In the bow, the eaglet flopped under the windbreaker in the inch of water on the canoe's floor.

From the corner of her eye, off to the distant south, a boat sped along the channel. Maybe it was the Naatucks and her father. Once they returned to the cabin, they'd find her gone and come looking. Come rescue her. Suddenly she realized she'd left her life jacket on the island. She could swim, but . . .

Another wave crested ahead, taller than the others. Alex dug harder into the lake with her paddle. She tried to keep the bow forward, straight on with the wave, but the canoe twisted. As Alex lifted her paddle, a wave hit, sprayed water across her whole body and into the canoe, and yanked the paddle from her grip.

"Oh no!" she cried as the paddle slipped over the next wave and became a mere twig in the distance.

She swore. Twice, then a third time.

Then she screamed.

But it did no good. Her paddle was gone.

The canoe turned broadside to the waves, taking on more water. Her weight made the canoe unstable. She slid to the floor and sat in water. Then she began paddling frantically with her hands, trying to turn the canoe into the wind, just to keep it from flooding. Her hands became rudders, bad ones, but better than nothing. What she needed most she didn't have.

Thunder boomed, rib-racking loud, and lightning

followed less than a second after, flashing across the sky to the north. Again thunder rumbled, this time low in the belly of a great beast as it grumbled out in a series of deafening booms. Alex braced herself. She was a perfect target. Again lightning crackled the sky, ripping its way through a fabric of murky gray. If eagles were smart, they'd build their homes in caves, not in the highest treetops.

Another wave plowed into the canoe, spinning it broadside again. Alex hung on, paddled hard on her right, struggling to counter its force.

Beneath the bow seat, the eaglet flopped in the water, his talon tangled in the string of Alex's jacket's hood. His soaked tail feathers protruded from under the edge of the windbreaker.

Her windbreaker. Her brilliant plan gone wrong. Gone afoul. *A fowl.* A pun. As if there were anything funny about her situation.

What a disaster she'd created. This poor eaglet. Half drowning in a canoe with a broken wing was the last thing he deserved. Her chest felt heavy with regret. She had only wanted to help the eaglet, to prove herself to her father. But what had she proved?

Waves pushed the canoe faster than she could have paddled it. The wind carried it along, nearly picking it up and out of the water at times before setting it upon the crest of another wave that pushed it farther and farther from the Naatucks' cabin.

Two seagulls flew over the canoe, perhaps to scavenge a leftover lunch or whatever a fisherman might toss overboard, then moved on.

"Nothing here," Alex called up, the wind snatching her words. "And we're not dead yet!"

The birds flew higher and headed north.

She blinked back water. Time slowed, marked only by the rhythm of the waves, the high-pitched humming of the wind. Head down, Alex tried to keep a lookout for the paddle. The chances of getting it back were slim. But with the wind pushing the canoe eastward, perhaps the paddle was close by, traveling at the same speed. She kept using her hands to steady the canoe. The lake numbed her hands, absorbed her warmth, and iced her body. She trembled and her teeth began to chatter.

Something shimmered near the canoe. The paddle. She wasn't going to let it slip by. She cupped her hands tighter and scooped water, trying to nudge the canoe toward the shape. Before the next wave snatched it from her, she reached for the flat of the paddle. Her hand clenched fast around something cold. Something slippery and squishy.

She winced—"Oh! Puh-lease!"—and drew her hand back into the canoe, then, on second thought, let her hand trail in the water outside the canoe, hoping to wash off the slime. A dead and bloated fish floated off on the next wave.

She groaned.

The eaglet had stopped struggling, but now he held

himself upright, feet planted in the water, his body cloaked in blue and teal. When a wave hit, he scrambled to steady himself, tried to reach around with his head, sometimes knocking against the wall of the canoe and falling. Alex hated watching him lose his balance and flail to gain footing, but there was nothing she could do.

She ached inside, hated how terribly stupid and helpless and alone she felt. Tears welled up and merged with rain down her face. Before anyone would notice or figure she was missing, she and the eaglet would probably be at the bottom of the lake or floating, food for scavengers.

If she died, would she be with her brother? She always pictured him in a good place, somewhere happy and without suffering. Was there such a place, a heaven, for him? If she died, would there ever be a heaven for her?

In every direction, there was too much water. Rocking, churning, waves of water.

And no cell phone. No emergency phones. No policemen or rangers. Nobody to help.

Water clouded her vision, dripped off her nose, and soaked her skin. She sank lower, continuing to use her hands as rudders, using her body to counter the waves' unceasing efforts to turn the canoe and its cargo upside down. For hours, beneath dark thunderheads, the canoe rode foamy waves, swiftly floating eastward. Alex felt pushed forward by forces beyond her control in a tiny green vessel on miles and miles and miles of empty, wind-churned water.

CHAPTER SEVEN

Alone

All the rain, the steady pounding incessant rain, made her think of the playhouse. For years, she had managed not to think about it, not to remember anything. A thought would flicker in her mind and before it would come fully to life she'd snuff it out, like a candle extinguisher over a hungry flame.

The playhouse. She didn't have the strength now, and the waves and water and rhythmic rocking lulled her. She let the memory come.

Her father had built it, and it had sat in the corner of the backyard, right beside the ginkgo tree. He worked from sketches Mom had drawn. He cut wood with his circular saw. It buzzed as he filled the air with the sweet scent of wood chips, a growing mound of vanilla-colored chips and sawdust that she and Jonathan played in. She used her brother's yellow front-end loader and dump truck, hauling wood chips with him, load by load, to the compost container.

When the playhouse was finished, her parents held a grand ceremony complete with a decorated cake. Abuela Elena arrived, her silver hair bobbed and bouncing, carrying a brightly colored homemade quilt. Alex taped a red ribbon across the door frame, then handed her grandma the scissors. "Abuelita, you're the oldest. You should cut the ribbon."

"*Gracias,*" her grandmother said with a broad smile. "I would be honored."

They had just moved to San Jose from Minnesota, so at first, Alex had played only with Jonathan in the cedar-shingled playhouse, complete with blue shutters, real flower boxes, and a red door. Inside, they sipped tea from plastic toy cups, toasted the queen and king, played bankers and robots and "chinny-chin-chin," Jonathan's shortened name for the Three Pigs and the Big Bad Wolf. He was always a pig; she was the wolf. And sometimes she fell asleep with him on the green folding cot under the orange-and-yellow quilt that always made her think of *churros*. Probably because Abuela Elena always made *churros*, puffy and hot and lightly sprinkled with sugar.

A shriek pulled her from her daydream.

In the bow, the eaglet flailed and kicked, a mangled mess of wing and tail feathers, beak and talons. Now its hood had come free and he was eyeing her, flopping in the water, half covered by her windbreaker. Alex drew her sandaled feet toward her and sat cross-legged. Her toes might look like easy food.

The eaglet continued to struggle, his body looking smaller and smaller as water saturated his feathers. And in an instant, he managed to shed the windbreaker and hop to the bow seat. He sank his talons into the woven seat and stared at her, as if to say, "Why?"

She sat against the stern seat in three or four inches of water that sloshed and sprayed with the waves. Another wave rolled into them and threatened to turn the canoe sideways. Alex paddled with her numb hands, straightening the canoe and turning it downwind.

The eaglet cocked his head, one eye on her, steady, unflinching, as if he could reach into her soul and read everything written there. Her thoughts, her fears, her secrets. The wind blew its brown crest feathers up.

"A mohawk," Alex said. "Very cool."

Another wave bounced them sideways and water flowed over the canoe's side.

"Just what we need," Alex said.

The eaglet's eyelid slid sideways and open again. Eagles didn't have regular eyelids. Instead, a thin membrane closed sideways across their eye like the quick shutter of a camera.

The eaglet rode that way, never taking his eye off her, despite the falling rain and the wind that howled around them, as if she were the one who had been captured, not the other way around. He stood guard, shaking like a sentry who had stood out in the cold too long. A sentry with a broken arm hanging awkwardly at his side.

Glancing in every direction, Alex hoped for any sign of boats. Whitecaps and sheets of slate-gray rain filled her view. She would simply have to wait it out. Wait for help. Wait until the canoe touched shore. At least she wasn't on the ocean. She had seen a map. The lake had its limits, even if it stretched eighty miles end to end. Even if it was a labyrinth of islands and channels.

"Labyrinth," she said aloud. An endless maze, that's what she was floating on. Once she found her way into it, could she find her way out again? She was glad the eaglet was with her. He was only a bird, but even his company was better than being completely alone. "Sentry," she said. And the eagle blinked sideways. "That's what I'm going to call you. You mind?"

Maybe if she talked to the eaglet, he would have a better chance of surviving and wouldn't try jumping into the lake. If she lost the eaglet, she couldn't bear it. "So chin up, huh? You and I, we're going to be just fine. Don't you worry your little eagle brain about anything, okay, Sentry?"

A chill had settled deep inside. Alex began to shiver uncontrollably. All that water. It was cooling her down to lake temperatures, which had to be about fifty below zero. Her teeth chattered and her body kept shuddering. More than anything, she wanted to be dry and warm. She didn't care if she ever got home again, if she could only get to some source of heat. Still, she kept her numb hands in the lake, ruddering the canoe, keeping it upright, letting the wind pass by on either side of port and starboard, not letting it swamp them.

The eaglet turned his head and studied her. He ruffled his feathers, puffing up only slightly.

"Maya said eagles . . . are a symbol of strength and wisdom." Her own lips weren't moving very well, but she kept talking. "She's Ojibwe, or at least part, and she would know. Maybe you were sent here by the Great Spirit to teach me something. That's what Maya would say."

Thunder and lightning passed on ahead, but a driving cold rain continued to push the canoe eastward. Alex tried to keep talking.

"My brother," she continued. "When he mile—" Her words weren't forming right on her lips. She tried again. "When he smiled," she said, "his eyes scrunched up and—" She stopped. Talking was too much work. Her brother. He had shared everything, even bites from his peanut-butter-and-jelly sandwiches. If she could go back in time, she'd lift him from the floor of the playhouse after the time he drank from her birthday tea set without her permission. She'd pushed him right off his little plastic chair. *He was great. Really, Sentry, you would have liked him.*

The canoe twisted and dipped, riding low in the water. It crested over the top of one wave and slid down into the valley of the next. Alex felt numb and limp. Any moment, the canoe would capsize, fill with water, and she would be too cold to hang on. She'd just slide into the lake and sleep.

Her stomach churned with all the endless up-and-down motion. She closed her eyes, clung to both sides of the canoe, and slid lower, her head tilted back against the seat, and cold rain fell on her face and eased her urge to throw up.

And still the canoe floated eastward.

Alex had no idea how much time had passed when the canoe bumped against rock, jolting her. She opened her eyes. To her amazement, the eaglet was still there, clinging to the seat.

When she tried to stand, her legs wouldn't obey. She felt confused. Couldn't remember why she was in the canoe. Slowly, as if they didn't belong to her, she lifted her hands before her eyes. Water puckered. Grayish-blue. Rain fell steadily. She didn't care. All she wanted was to sleep, just to lie down in the water in the canoe and sleep.

With a shriek, the eaglet startled her. Awkwardly he

flapped one wing, then hopped from his seat to the bow, to shore, and was gone. She had to follow him.

Alex forced herself to move. Slowly she pushed herself over the seat, the yoke, the bow, and stepped onto a large boulder, her legs shaking so badly that her knees buckled. She fell, but felt nothing.

A large spruce tree darkened the edge of the woods. Its long branches swept the floor. Shelter. Dry shelter. Alex half walked, half crawled. She eased herself under the spruce's prickly arms. Near its trunk, on a dry patch of ground, she drew her knees to her chest and closed her eyes.

Somewhere, Nowhere

Strange, that feeling of waking, or nearly waking, of hovering between the gray and cozy place of dream and thought before opening your eyes to reality. Alex knew this place. She wondered if she was dreaming, or remembering.

"Better pump her stomach," said one.

"Why on earth do teenagers do this to themselves?"

"She may have had no idea what she was doing."

"Let's hope she didn't."

"Okay, IV's in. . . ."

"*Gracias*, Conway."

Conway. She didn't know a Conway. Maybe she was

dreaming. Her eyes wouldn't open. She wanted to open them.

Before, in this place of gray, she'd heard her mother's voice.

"Honey? Alex? Sweetheart. Whatever happened, we can talk about it later. Right now, I'm so mad, I could kill you. I won't, of course, but why on earth . . . Just wake up and I'll feel better. Just squeeze my hand. There. That's good. We'll talk later."

And a nurse had talked with her as she swabbed warm cotton around the edges of Alex's mouth. Probably to remove some embarrassing crusty drool. "You have two parents who love you, Alexis," the nurse said, her voice sweet as maple syrup. Light played behind Alex's eyes— daylight? she wondered—-still, she kept her eyes shut. She wasn't ready to meet anyone else's eyes. "They've been calling and coming in," the nurse continued, "making my life pretty difficult, actually. You're a lucky girl, you know that? Lucky to have parents who come to see you. Lucky to be alive this mornin'."

When the room was quiet again, Alex opened her eyes. She was alone in a white room. A painting of a pastel, speckled landscape hung across from her hospital bed. She looked out the window. Palm trees edged the parking lot below. Sun shone through a morning mist carried from the bay. She pretended for a moment that she was in a hotel with room service, but that didn't last long.

Her father walked in. "Alexis," he said, suddenly towering at the foot of her bed. In his large tan hands he held a plush toy eagle. Unceremoniously he tossed it on the end of her bed. If he was going to come all this way, why couldn't he just come as her father? The stuffed toy eagle just reminded her that he was Dr. Reed, Eagle Expert. He had likely picked it off his bookshelf, a gift someone had given him. She was too old for stuffed toys, anyway. He still saw her as eight years old, not thirteen. She turned away, angry.

"Hey, don't act so happy to see me," he said.

Alex couldn't answer. She pulled the sheet up over her shoulder, realizing she was in a thin cotton nightgown that tied in the back. Strange, knowing you hadn't put on a piece of clothing you were wearing. Who had?

His weight sank a corner of her bed as he sat. Alex moved her feet. She felt tears building behind her eyes. She wasn't going to cry. She needed to keep her emotions in control. That's what he liked best.

He drew a breath. "First, I'm glad to see you're okay— I mean, at least physically. Binge drinking like that. You could have killed yourself."

"Maybe that's what I wanted." Alex flung the words at him. She was shocked at herself, but now the words were out.

"Hey, let's not talk crazy, now," he said. He shifted and patted the sheet about her feet.

Alex kicked the sheet away.

"Oh—you won't give me a chance, will you?" He huffed, stood, stepped to the window. "What? What is at the bottom of all this, anyway? Is it the new friends your mother told me about? Getting your belly button pierced? What is it, Alex?" His voice was harsh now, over the edge. "Have you figured it out for yourself yet?"

Alex rolled over, turned her back on him. Wanting him to leave, wanting him to sit back down and try again, to rest his hand softly on her shoulder. To say something more, something she needed to hear from him.

"Listen," he whispered. "I have to catch a flight soon. We can make good use of this time, or I can leave." She felt his hand on her blanketed shoulder, patting.

She pulled away.

He sighed. "Guess I'll go, if that's what you want."

For a few seconds, his words hovered there. Alex didn't want to have to speak. She wanted him to be her father, to know that she needed more than a lecture right then. Anger and tears churned in her throat. She couldn't answer.

"Okay, then," he said. "You're okay. That's what counts. Um . . . I have to give a lecture this evening in Minneapolis. So—bye, honey." His footsteps faded with his words, and he was gone.

Later, breakfast arrived on a cart: covered dishes holding oatmeal and scrambled eggs, orange juice and hot tea. Alex had never been so hungry. After saturating her body with alcohol, she should have been too sick to eat. But the stomach pumping must have handled that problem. She was sore, achy, and famished. She inhaled her food.

"You're a ravenous bird," the hospital aide said, pointing, "just like your eagle there."

"It's not my—"

He winked at her and stepped out of the room, tray in hands.

That's when her mother stepped in, almost as if on cue. Her father steps out, she steps in. They must have planned it that way. Avoid each other at all times; that was their policy. "I took the day off. I'm here until they discharge you." She pushed her hair off her shoulders. In her stretch blouse and jeans, her mother appeared young—but the darkness and puffiness beneath her eyes told Alex her mother hadn't slept.

"I'm sorry," Alex said, her voice cracking. "I don't know why I did what I did."

Her mom's chin quivered. "That's okay, Alex. We really don't have to talk now if you don't want."

"Mom, I wanted to get drunk. I mean, it wasn't just for fun. It was like I was, I don't know—" She glanced away, studied the painting, then finally met her mom's eyes. "Angry. At everything, I think. At you, for going to Pismo Beach. I mean, you left me to stay with people I barely know, and . . . we had our tradition—"

"I'm sorry about that," her mom said.

"But—does that mean I'm . . . an alcoholic or something?"

Her mom shook her head, reached out, placed her hand on Alex's bare wrist. It felt warm, good. Alex didn't move her arm away.

"No, you're not an alcoholic—not by drinking once. It's the *why* I'm concerned about. It's the *why* you need to think about, too. Why did you want to get drunk? What were you angry about? What were you running from? Was it pressure from your new group of friends, or more than that?"

"Hey, my friends are fine, Mom. I know they're not perfect, like Mercedes, but I never told you this—as soon as I got first chair, she stopped calling me. Shut me out. I mean, what kind of a friend is that? She's more interested in competing, being the best at everything, than being a real friend, anyway. I couldn't talk with her about anything anymore."

"Sometimes," her mother continued, turning her head and looking out the window. She fingered her top shirt button. "Sometimes the loneliness gets to me, too," her mom said. "Without Jonathan. Without your father, even though I know deep down that we don't know how to be together anymore. Everything changed from when we first met at UCLA." She paused and gazed out the window. "But bottom line? I wish, now, that I had stayed home and that we'd kept our breakfast tradition. I could have gone later, but Oscar was so excited about taking his boat out of the marina early in the morning while the boat activity was low."

"So, did he?"

"Well," her mom began, then smiled. "He had bilge problems at the last minute."

For a second, Alex laughed. Then her nose tingled, that feeling that came just before crying. Her mom leaned closer, touched forehead to forehead, just as Alex's tears began to flow. "I love you, Alex. I really do."

Behind Alex's eyes, gray light settled into darkness again. The chatter of an angry squirrel sounded from above, scolding. The ground prickled beneath her side. She couldn't place herself in time. She needed to move, to get up. But she couldn't open her eyes. Couldn't connect her brain to her arms or legs or eyelids. She needed to rest on this downy cushion of gray nothing. Gradually, caught between two worlds, she drifted back to something like sleep.

CHAPTER NINE

Stranded

Mosquitoes buzzed in a thick cloud around Alex in her dreams. They landed on her face, crawled on her lips and neck and hands. With delicate wings, they hovered, like unwanted memories, then landed on skin, lifting their thin needles and penetrating to draw blood.

Alex couldn't wake. She tried to brush them away, but her arms wouldn't move. Curled on her side in a tight ball, she slipped deeper into sleep.

Sometime later, a sharp smell—like rotten meat or cat-urine-soaked carpet—reached her nose. Where was she, anyway? Dreaming, most likely. Something wet touched her nose and snorted. It shuffled beside her. A beast of some sort? A wild dog? Her mind began to make connections. Adrenaline shot through her and she opened her eyes.

A bear. Shadowed by the tree, its bulk was a boulder in the gray light.

Alex blinked.

The bear shifted back and forth on its legs and swayed its head. Its coat was reddish-brown, and though it wasn't huge, like grizzlies she'd seen in movies, it wasn't a tiny cub, either. It bayed at her, probably deciding if she was dead enough to eat yet or not. She might be its meal if she didn't move, do something.

A scream rose from her mouth, hoarse and unconvincing. She swallowed, tried again, and this time let out a high-pitched cry. She stared at the bear and yelled, "Get away from me!"

The bear tipped onto its rear, front paws up, seemingly baffled for a moment. Then it pivoted and disappeared. Brush rustled in its wake, and soon the woods around her grew silent, almost.

Alex felt herself drifting back toward sleep. She had to get up, get moving. What was this in her that made her just want to sleep? Sleeping sickness? Hypothermia? Was it possible she had been too cold and wet for too long? Maybe you didn't need to be in winter weather to get it.

Mosquitoes, she realized now, were humming, lighting on her neck and face. She brushed them away, her limbs thick and distant from her body.

Stand, she told herself, and eased forward onto her knees. She felt fear build in her like a wave, a wave that could gather momentum quickly and crest in a full-blown panic attack. She used to get them at every violin recital, shaking so badly that she could barely keep her fingers on the strings. Threw up once backstage, right before stepping onto the community center stage. She couldn't let it happen now. "There are times," she remembered her dad saying, "when your emotions can sabotage you. Times when you have to keep a level head and think—what do I need to do next to get out of this situation?"

For weeks after they'd returned to their house following earthquake tremors, she'd wake up crying. Her dad would come to her room and talk to her, patting her shoulder until she quieted, staying with her until she fell back asleep. She had completely panicked the first time she'd felt tremors—of course, she was only in second grade then—and he tried to explain what to do in a crisis. Don't panic, he'd instructed. This wasn't the time for emotion.

Alex rose heavily to her feet and stumbled through branches toward gray light. She leaned against the trunk of a Norway pine. She listened for the bear. Wind blew lightly through the overhead pine boughs. Frogs peeped. Beyond the edge of water was another shore, with a thin channel of water between the two peninsulas. Where was she? The wind had blown her eastward across water. Was she near mainland, and if so, was she in the United States or Canada? Near a road? She could try to get a ride.

She stepped away from the tree toward the rocky shore. Boulders were strewn along its edge, like a child's discarded marbles. The western sky was chalked grayish purple with a dab of red.

Suddenly panic lit in her. The sun had set already? So far north, it set around ten o'clock or so. She must have drifted on the lake for hours and slept even longer under the spruce. She rubbed her hand on her forehead and smeared mosquitoes beneath her palm. When she pulled away her hand, blood covered it. They had been feeding on her for hours. Her eyelids felt heavy, puffy. She had to—what? Where was she going to go to get help for herself? She had to canoe back, just keep paddling west until she found cabin lights. She couldn't spend the night out here, wherever "here" was, and survive.

Something crawled along the outer edge of her ear. She grabbed it between her thumb and forefinger and peered closely. It was the diameter of a pencil eraser. "A wood tick!" She flung it. How many did she have crawling on her now, embedding their little heads in her skin? She flinched, wrapped her arms across her chest tightly, and shouted, "Help! Someone help me!"

Bouncing back and forth across the channel, the echo sounded. "Someone help me, help me, me, me, me. . . ."

She studied the shoreline for the green canoe. Where

was it? She remembered now, vaguely, crawling out over the bow and heading for shelter. She hadn't tied it up. Like a little child, she hadn't looked back and thought about that, not for a moment. She really must have been out of it. Her father's words clanged again in her mind, "If your head's in the clouds today, Alex, you're going to get hurt." If there was ever a time for her to focus and think, it was now.

Alex scanned the shore, the shadowy underbrush. She saw no signs of the eaglet, either.

She swatted a mosquito on her neck, then another on her nose. She had no canoe and no idea where she was. In the increasing darkness, she could easily get more lost, if that were possible. She had to make a plan, do something.

Her only hope was to find a cabin. Some were abandoned and left to the park, others were still inhabited by families for a few more years until their leases ran out. She would follow the shoreline, stay along the water's edge. That way someone, someday, might find her. She'd keep moving until she found shelter. And maybe she'd find the canoe. Perhaps the wind had carried it—eastward.

Just follow the shoreline left, away from the setting sun. Alex's legs obeyed. They were stiff and unsteady, but they moved her forward. She kept them moving, first over moss-covered boulders. Then she followed the shore, and bare boulders gave way to a sandy cove. She ducked beneath branches and crawled over downed trees. It was a sandy shore that made the chances of finding a cabin even greater. She kept going, scanning the growing shadows for the eaglet and her canoe. Nothing.

Something squawked, a gravelly startled cry, just yards ahead of her. Alex froze and her heart rattled. The silhouette of a heron, its long neck and long legs extended, rose and flapped away from shore. She'd seen herons before along the ocean, nothing to be afraid of. She willed herself to keep moving.

She didn't want to startle anything else, especially another bear. The thought of it filled her with dread. Hadn't she heard it was good to make noise, to let a bear know you're coming so it wouldn't be startled? She needed a song, something cheery to lift her spirits. Her old friend Mercedes's favorite piece, "Ode to Joy," Beethoven. A song Alex knew by heart on her violin. She began to hum loudly, turning up the volume not only to fend off bears, but to give herself courage. She hummed, working her way down shore in near darkness, her hand becoming a flyswatter as she walked.

The shoreline grew wider, as if someone had cleared some of the brush back from shore, and she stepped up onto a board. A dock. She was standing on the edge of a dock! A short dock, granted, with no sign of boats around (or her canoe, for that matter), but a dock meant a cabin. And sure enough, to her left, only a dozen yards from the dock, lay a squat cabin, its shape black and beckoning.

Shelter. At least she might find a way to survive the night.

The cabin seemed to call to her, and she walked toward it. She couldn't even make out a door until she was nearly at the steps.

"Hello?" she called. "Anybody here? Hello?"

No answer.

Alex turned the knob, expecting resistance, but it turned freely, clicked open, and she stepped inside. She didn't want to close the door behind her, but if she didn't, her shelter would soon fill with mosquitoes. She pushed the door shut, leaned her back against it, and waited. Listened. What if someone was sleeping? An old hermit? A gun-crazy maniac?

She heard breathing, in and out, loud and steady. She listened hard, her heart racing ahead of her mind again, sending her into a panic. If she just turned around, grabbed the handle, and bolted out. . . . The breathing, she realized, matched her own. The breathing *was* her own.

"Oh, jeez!" She felt stupid.

She groped, hoping to find a light switch on the walls. Nothing to her right. To her left, fabric—a curtain, maybe—but no light switch. The Naatucks had electricity at their cabin, powered by cables that ran underwater from the mainland to their island. But this cabin was probably too far away.

For a long time, Alex stood still. The eaglet. Would the bear eat him? They were known to prey on eaglets. Guilt pressed in around her as thick as the darkness. Not only had she caused the eaglet's injury, but now she had completely abandoned him. By morning, if she was still alive, she'd search for him. She promised herself. Then when she was rescued, the eaglet would be, too.

She moved toward the curtains and found a pulley string. The curtains opened to darkness and stars as thick as snowflakes. She never thought stars could bring such comfort, but seeing them beyond the glass like that, suddenly she didn't feel quite so alone. They shimmered in the darkness, and just above the treetops on the opposite shore, greenish-white lights began to dance and glow. At first the lights were faint, soft paintbrush strokes of light, but then they deepened to neon green and pulsed, shooting upward like streams of lava. They had to be northern lights.

The illuminated sky cast a bright light into the cabin. Alex took in her surroundings. A square table and two chairs sat by a stone fireplace. The floor was thick with dirt. A wooden dresser and double bed with blankets filled one corner; a sink, a small stove, and a metal bucket stood in the other corner. On the wall near the door hung a jacket and a few wool shirts. Beneath the clothes lay a couple of pairs of boots.

As quickly as the northern lights had brightened, they faded, as if someone had turned down a dimmer switch. Alex stopped thinking. Her body knew what to do. She stripped out of her damp clothes, pulled a wool shirt off its peg, put it on, then went to the bed and crawled under heavy blankets.

Her body shivered violently, but gradually relaxed as faint heat built under the blankets. The air was musty and the wool made her nose itch. She watched the northern lights, now milky-white above the treetops, and wished she'd locked the door. A faint skittering sounded in the walls or on the roof, but Alex tried not to think, tried *hard* not to think, and soon fell asleep.

CHAPTER TEN

Beneath Dark Rafters

In muddy light, Alex woke to a thousand mice scritching and scratching somewhere in the cabin. Tiny claws on wood. She opened one eye, just enough to focus on a stone fireplace, frayed curtains opened to a square window, a small table, the one-room cabin she'd found last night.

Then she slept hard and woke much later to sunshine. The air was warm—sweetly putrid—waking her fully. Her nose began to itch again, and she scratched it. She felt crawly everywhere. The wool blankets. Wool always made her itchy.

The cabin was spare, built and furnished at a time when electricity probably wasn't even around. A partial ceiling covered the beams above her bed. The striped wool blankets were chewed and scattered with tiny black mouse droppings.

If she had to, she could probably catch mice for Sentry. She spotted a mousetrap beneath the sink. It held the tiny white bones of a mouse, nothing more.

On the wooden table sat a chipped, brown ceramic mug and a hefty layer of dust. No phone here, that was for certain. Not even a clock.

Maya had said that years back, when more Ojibwe than whites traveled the lake, cabin owners kept their doors unlocked to offer shelter to whoever was in need of it. If someone fell through the ice, they could warm themselves. If someone had to get out of a storm, there was always shelter nearby. That's why she and Ned didn't lock their doors now, which seemed foolish when Alex first heard Maya explain it. "Up here," she'd said, "you never know when someone might need shelter."

Still, she wanted an upgrade.

Clean sheets, a hot tub, and room service.

She'd have to talk with the manager.

Climbing out from under the blankets, she surveyed the red-and-black plaid wool shirt that hung to her knees. On her bare legs were a dozen brownish-black wood ticks. "Oh—oh—oh!" She hated wood ticks, with their little beady heads, flat and round bodies, their little legs that wiggled from their edges. She pulled at one, firmly fastened on the inside of her knee. It came free, a small flake of white skin in its mouth. "I'm gonna die, I'm gonna go crazy!"

Tick after tick after tick. Alex grabbed one, flung it to the floor, then grabbed another. Thirteen, just from her legs. She hated to explore the rest of her body. Her stomach turned on itself, empty with hunger, sick with the thought of wood ticks crawling all over her body through the night. They must have found her when she was under the spruce tree—passed out, pretty much, for hours.

Passed out. Seemed to be her talent lately. If her friends were here, at least they might laugh with her. Her friends would shriek with excitement, cry for each other, listen when you were hurting. Not like Mercedes, who believed that a week was long enough to feel blue about anything. After that, "you should set new goals. Get over it." But Alex hadn't been able to get over how she felt, especially not in so short a time. So when Sky-Li confided that she sometimes felt so lonely that she'd wrap her arms around herself just to get a hug, Alex in turn had confessed that when she was feeling sad, she slept with her brother's old baby blanket, buried her nose in its familiar smell, and cried. When morning came, she hid it on the top shelf of her closet. Right now, she needed the kind of friend who was there for you, no matter what.

Alex removed the wool shirt and hung it on the back of the chair. Then she studied herself in the hazy mirror above the sink. Lifting her hair, she checked her neck, found two more wood ticks, and flung them to the floor. She felt for ticks behind her ears, found five, and yanked those from her flesh. She checked her armpits, her belly button—and discovered a wood tick behind the edge of the lavender bead on the silver ring. "Gross!"

The skin around one end of the belly ring was scraped red from getting caught on the eagles' nest. She'd never understood why her father got so upset about the ring, but if he'd warned her about climbing with it, she might have removed it ahead of time. He should have been more upset about exposing her to wood ticks. If she were bitten by a deer tick, she might get Lyme disease, a truly serious illness that made people sick for a long, long time. She studied her body for any red rings, bull's-eye marks, the telltale sign of a Lyme infection. Her ankles and wrists were red from scratching. Her lips and eyelids were swollen from mosquito or gnat bites. A red gash sliced diagonally across her shin, and her palms were black with pitch and dirt.

Aside from all that, she was alive. She laughed out loud. "What a sight!"

The dirt was thick beneath her bare feet, and when she looked closer, she realized it wasn't dirt. It was droppings from mice. Except the droppings ran in dry rows, about a foot apart, columns of droppings.

Reluctantly Alex looked up. In the shadows of the rafter beams, wedged in thick rows between the beams and roof, were dozens—no—hundreds of bats.

Snatching the wool shirt, she darted for the door, jumping between rows of bat guano. She jumped to the top step into the bright sunlight. Naked. As fast as she could, she pulled the wool shirt over her bare skin and gulped air. So *that* was what all the scratching had been in the gray dawn hours. Like vampires coming in before the light of day, the bats must have been returning from their night hunt before the sun rose.

There was absolutely no way she was going to spend another minute, let alone another night in that cabin. To think that she'd slept the whole night in there with all those bats stretching and fanning their thin, leathery wings overhead. And now, she'd stupidly flung all thirty-seven wood ticks on the floor. She hadn't been thinking, of course. If she had to sleep in that bed another night, the ticks would find her, crawl up to the bed. . . .

She wouldn't stay. That's all there was to it. She had to get help, get rescued. Simple.

A droning of dragonflies filled the air. Large red-bodied dragonflies and smaller bright-blue dragonflies whirred like tiny helicopters, darting after tiny bugs. "Eat every mosquito you find," Alex said. "Show no mercy." Bats, too, ate mosquitoes, but that didn't mean she had to like them.

Her stomach rumbled, reminding her that she had eaten only a bowl of cereal since yesterday morning. If she could only find the canoe, she could get her backpack and food. Then she remembered. She'd left her backpack on Skipper Rock.

Alex pressed her fingertips across her lips. Long grasses covered the short distance from cabin to dock. The beach was sandy; the dock was half rotted away, its farthest end dipping into the lake, creating a mossy platform where a painted turtle now sat, its head slightly angled up out of its shell. Turtle soup, if she got desperate.

Not only was she hungry, but she was dying of thirst. The water looked so good. She didn't have water tablets along to purify the water. She didn't need to get—what was it? Giardia? She didn't need to get sick along with being lost. Alex stepped from the cabin toward the water.

At her movement, the turtle slipped off its perch into the lake. Beyond the dock by about twenty yards lay another shore, its bank as steep and high as her cove was flat and sandy. Such sharp contrasts in terrain. About as different as her father was from her mother.

And she was like the water that flowed between the two shores. The thing that still bound her parents together. The reason they hadn't gotten the divorce yet, and why they had been separated for three years without taking the next step. She wished they'd just get it over with. Who were they fooling? Not her. That was for sure.

A breeze blew in between the two landmasses and the channel. She needed to know where she was. Needed to find the eaglet. Needed her clothes.

Reluctantly she stepped back to the cabin, command-ing herself not to look up at the rafters. The air was grow-ing riper now, warmed by the sunshine that revealed a floor covered with inches of dried bat dung. She'd heard of caves that had been excavated for tons and tons of bat dung, which was then sold and shipped as fertilizer. Really, this wasn't as bad as it could be.

Alex grabbed her still damp sandals and clothes, hus-tled back outside, and put them on. She wore everything. She didn't need to donate any more blood to mosquitoes. First, find Sentry, who would need medical care as soon as possible. Then, find out if there was any sign of life near-by, someone to help them both get back.

She wandered past the shed behind the cabin and fol-lowed the shoreline eastward. Not far from the cabin, in the center of a web built between two cedars, hung an orange spider, startling as a bright, fat jewel. After the bear, bats, and wood ticks, Alex wasn't even scared. But she didn't want to get too close, either. She didn't think there were any poisonous spiders in Minnesota (or Canada—wherever she was), but she didn't want to find out the hard way that she was wrong. She skirted the web, stepping deeper into the woods, and crossed a small stream that flowed to the shore.

Since the island appeared to be a thin layer of soil and greenery over rock, the stream had to flow from its own source. A natural spring. The stream ran clear over rocks and moss. It should be good for drinking. She followed the stream deeper into the woods and finally found a clear pool of water, only three feet wide and deep, where water flowed, pooled, and trickled over an edge downward toward the lake. Alex cupped her hands and dipped them in the water. Nothing swam or darted that she could see. It looked good enough to drink, and she did. Water had never tasted so good. She drank deeply, again and again, until she was satisfied. She'd found a good source of drinking water. If she needed to, she could return to this spot easily.

The island, as she came to discover, was a good hike from end to end. For at least an hour, she followed its shoreline looking for Sentry, but saw no sign of him. Eventually she climbed a steep embankment on the island's northwest corner, kicking up mosquitoes from their rain-dampened leafy shelters.

Out of breath, Alex reached the island's topmost crest, a slab of lichen-crusted rock, arching like a humpback whale. Pink wild roses bloomed from crevices. In every direction, islands dotted the horizon. From what she could tell, her island was shaped like a giant kidney bean, rocky all around except for the sandy beach in its concave center, where someone had once wisely located a cabin. Across from her island, the neighboring island rose steeply above the narrow channel, but from end to end, it was skinny and short as a well-used pencil. She'd name them. Kidney Bean Island and Pencil Island.

To the north, to the south, tiny islands dotted the lake. Her island was part of a cluster of islands—an archipelago, now, that was a good word—on Rainy Lake. She shaded her eyes and tried to spot a slick green pea-pod shape—the canoe—but no luck. The canoe was gone. It had either floated to one side of the island or right through the channel and out again to open water. And Sentry had vanished.

She had started down the sloping rock toward the island's western point when a sharp cry, piercing and sad, filled the air. She looked up at the clear sky, so changed from the stormy day before. No eagles circled overhead. She looked around. The cry had to have come from Sentry. But where was he?

Alex raced downhill toward the tall spruce closest to the island's western point, the tree where she had rested. She saw him before she reached it. In a small clearing, on the high end of a downed pine tree, perched the eaglet. He sat about four feet off the ground, watching her. Since he clearly couldn't fly, he must have picked his way up the log to its highest point.

"Sentry," Alex said apologetically. "You okay?"

The eaglet didn't move a feather. His right wing hung limp at his side; his left wing was tucked up securely beside his body where it should be. In the full sunlight, his brown feathers appeared dry. At least he had managed to survive so far. No thanks to her. Now she had to make sure he stayed alive.

Sentry studied her with his black eye. Alex wished he could talk. She wished they could put their heads together and figure out what to do next.

Her stomach sounded off, almost like the heron she'd startled the night before.

The eaglet opened his beak, dark except for the yellow painted at the edges of his mouth.

"Hungry?" Alex said, pushing her hands into her nearly dry pants pockets. "That makes two of us."

The eaglet closed his beak, then opened it wide again.

A white-throated sparrow broke into song somewhere on the island.

"So, what time is breakfast? How often do your parents feed you? What do they feed you?" Her father said adult eagles fed mostly fish to the eaglets, sometimes breaking up the fish into small, bite-size pieces. The eaglet kept watching her, as if waiting to hear her plan. She let out a breath.

"Until we get rescued or find a way out of here, I better come up with something for us to eat, huh?" She glanced around. Blueberries, she already knew, weren't going to be in abundance. A few yards off, red berries clung to low plants, just beneath overhanging bushes. Alex stepped closer to examine them. They were wild strawberries, a fraction of the size of those found at the supermarket. She picked them one at a time and popped each berry—sweet and ripe—into her mouth. She hadn't seen many on her hike around the island, but she could look more earnestly, if she had to.

An overhanging bush with thorny stems and tiny white flowers caught her eye. A raspberry bush, but its fruit was far from ripe. She would have to become a survivalist. Dad would be proud. He'd always said a person could survive in the wild if they were resourceful. If she was forced to, she'd live on strawberries, chokecherries, thimbleberries, cattail roots, and even rose-hip tea. But Sentry couldn't survive on those things. He was a carnivore, not a vegetarian.

"Well, little guy," she said, "looks like we're going to have to catch some fish. But I should warn you. When it comes to fishing, my track record isn't good." She looked from the eaglet to the lake, a long stretch of grayish-blue that seemed to extend forever. When she used to fish with her dad, her mind wandered from what she was doing. Once he caught her daydreaming with the minnow hovering above the water. "Hoping for a fish to jump up and put itself on that hook?" he'd asked jokingly. He was partly right about her head being in the clouds. She did have a tendency to daydream.

Sentry stared, standing on yellow legs, his talons clenching rotten wood. He seemed friendly. Distant and cautious, yes. He was a wild bird. She didn't expect to turn him into a pet. Still, he wasn't acting threatened by her presence. He was, after all, only six weeks old. Whether he cared for her or not didn't really matter. At least he tolerated her. What she needed to figure out was how to take care of him.

He opened his beak wide again.

"I know, I know," she said. "I promised to take care of you—and I will." She fixed a steady gaze back at the eaglet. Somehow she was going to have to think like a grown eagle.

CHAPTER ELEVEN

Castaway

As she tried to figure out how to catch a fish for the eaglet—and for herself—she wondered if Sentry had managed to eat anything since the night before. Probably not. After all, so far in his short life, all he had to do was sit in his nest and wait for food to appear magically. The thought stopped her and she smiled.

"Sort of like me," she confessed. Wasn't that pretty much what she did? Wait for her mother to serve up dinner? Once in a while Alex cooked macaroni and cheese or enchiladas, when her mom was really tight for time and coming home late after a real-estate deal. But mostly, her mom served great food, from fajitas to grilled lemon-pepper chicken to sautéed mushrooms and guava-banana salad. And the more Alex ate, the happier her mom seemed. Not that her mom wanted her to be fat, just well fed. Alex imagined that she would feel a similar satisfaction once she fed her starving eaglet.

The drone of a boat motor suddenly registered. A boat, puttering through the channel. She hadn't been listening for it, hadn't heard it until just that moment. A boat! Its sound floated up from the water and passed the point, not more than fifty yards away. She caught a glimpse of it through the trees. A flash of blue, two men with caps. Not the Naatucks' boat. The boat motored slowly, as if avoiding rocks or looking for someone. Of course. Her!

"Wait there," Alex told Sentry. She almost expected him to answer her, to nod in reply. "I didn't expect we'd be found so soon!'

She tore through the woods, not caring if branches scraped her hands and wrists, and headed to the shoreline. The sun was high and hot in the sky, and the ground nearly steamed with scents of cedar, pine, and earth. The inboard motor rumbled, and the boat cruised slowly down the channel toward the cabin, its wake white and frothy.

Alex grabbed the trunk of a cedar that leaned out over the water, hoping they would see her. She waved her arms and shouted. "Over here!" she called. "Here I am!"

The boat slowed at the dock, and two men stood up behind the windshield of their blue-and-gray motorboat, its name scrolled in white letters on its stern: *Castaway*.

Her life as a castaway was going to be short-lived. Thank goodness.

She let go of the cedar and ran along the shoreline, ducking in and out of branches, scrambling over three fallen trees. Boulders rose from the shore, blocking a direct route, but she either climbed over them or around them. Amazing that she had made it along the shore at all the night before. She had been out of her head with sleepiness and cold, but the bear had nudged her into enough panic to wake up. Now she could at least see where she was going. She neared the sandy cove and emerged from the woods. Thank God she wouldn't have to sleep there another night.

"Nobody here!" one of the men shouted above the motor, his voice clear as a trumpet over the water.

"Hey!" Alex shouted, waving her arms at them, running along the sand.

"Let's keep moving!" the other shouted. "Who knows where that kid may have landed. Could be a long day."

"Hey!" Alex cried, her voice hitting the air the same instant the man punched the motor into forward. "Hey!" she cried again, running along the sand shore, waving her arms, yelling. "I'm—over—*here*!"

The boat rumbled past the dock down the channel, picking up speed. In less than three seconds, Alex reached the dock, waving, calling, jumping. But the boat was gone, beyond the bend in the channel, heading out toward open water.

Her arms dropped at her sides. She sagged to a cross-legged position and watched the boat's wake fade in the channel. Beyond, the boat motor droned off—an angry bee to a hungry mosquito to the buzz of a gnat—until the air turned silent again. Silent, at least of human sounds, except for her heartbeat.

A search was under way for her. Her father and the Naatucks had come home last night, found her gone.

A search boat checked her island. Found no one. They moved on to other parts of the lake.

She exhaled, hard and sharp.

How long would it be before they checked here again? Another day or two. Maybe longer. The lake was endless. It went on and on forever.

She wanted to cry. Wanted to just give herself over to tears and sobbing. Just lie on the dock and give up completely.

Legs crossed, chin in her fists, she stared. The wake, like a jet stream lingering long after a plane has crossed the sky, remained. It curved at the bend in the channel, heading east where the searchers had gone. Soon the wake was merely ripples, and along the sandy shore, the last of the boat's waves rolled up softly, then fell silent.

CHAPTER TWELVE

Hunger

For several minutes, Alex sat on the dock, hoping that the boat would return. The sun beat down on her head and perspiration slid down her back in one slow bead. Finally she turned from the water and walked slowly along the sand beach back to Sentry.

A sharp crack sounded across from the sandy cove.

She jumped, blood rushing through her body. The bear—it must have returned.

Slap! She spun in the direction of the sound. Beside the opposite shore, a beaver glided through the channel, leaving behind a freshly fallen aspen tree on the bank, its branches lying in the water. The beaver climbed awkwardly up a sloping rock. It waddled a few paces, its round back glistening in the sun, then hid, a dark hump blending in with the shadows beneath balsam branches.

Alex paused and watched. The beaver clearly thought he was completely hidden, but she could make out his form. She waited for him to move, but he was so still, he must have decided to take a nap.

She glanced at the sun, slightly beyond its midway point in the sky. She had lots of hours left before nightfall. Two things. "First," she said aloud, holding up her pointer finger, "find something for Sentry—and me—to eat." Her father would be proud of her. She hadn't completely given herself over to emotion. She was thinking her way through this situation. "Second." She held up two fingers, which could be *peace* or *victory* or just *two*. "Look for a way off the island or a way to get help." She held up three fingers. Herself, her mother, her father. She slowly held up four fingers. And her brother. The way she wished things could be. Stupid. Of course, that could never be.

She followed the shoreline and caught herself shaking out her hands, the way she often did after practicing violin for an hour straight. That's what she needed, her violin. If she had to be stranded, like Robinson Crusoe, she wished she could at least play some music. "I hate to see you quit the violin, and I will respect your decision," her mom had said, "but you might have told me first before *pawning* it."

Pawning it. She felt bad for her violin now, thinking of

it, a Lewis Aristocrat, four simple strings stretched across maple-colored wood, sitting on a shelf among discarded electric guitars, stereos, and whatnot. The shopkeeper had seemed confused. "So, you don't want money, now?" he'd asked softly, examining her violin in his veiny white hands. "Let me get this straight. You won't leave me your name or number. You just want me to sell it and you'll come back later for the money?" Alex had nodded. By getting rid of it, she'd somehow thought she was putting a period at the end of a sentence, saying, *Stop*, or, *I've had enough*.

"It's a sweet little violin—you think about it," the shop-keeper called as the pawnshop door's bell jangled behind her. She ran to the corner and sat in the graffiti-decorated bus stop shelter. Before her city bus arrived, she was in tears. When she got home, she'd lied and told her mom that she'd lost her violin, which didn't go over big. And when Alex couldn't look her mother in the eyes, her mom said, "Okay, now the *real* story." Eventually, Alex confessed, right before catching a flight to Minnesota. The only person she'd hurt, she realized now, had been herself. If she ever made it home again, she'd see if her violin was there, waiting on the pawnshop shelf.

A flash of black and yellow—a garter snake—wove its way across the sand, only inches from her feet, and disappeared into the rushes at the edge of rocks and sand, startling Alex from her thoughts. She hurried back to the pine stump where Sentry had been perching. But Sentry was gone. Alex was filled with a frightening emptiness. "Where are you?" she called. Without the eaglet she'd truly be all alone.

Within a few breaths, she found him, a short distance away on the ground, flattening himself against a bed of spring-green moss and tiny white flowers.

"There you are," Alex said. She reached down and, without pausing from fear, she grabbed him, firmly yet gently, hands over his wings so he couldn't flap them. She eased him against her chest, talons safely outstretched away from her. Then, carefully watching her step, she carried him all the way back to the cabin. She needed to keep him from wandering from her sight and keep him quiet and contained so he wouldn't get hurt worse. He belonged in his nest at this age, not wandering around on the ground. The cabin was one possibility.

The shed leaned slightly toward the water, but it was still standing. It would be even better.

Through long grasses, Alex picked her way to the shed. Near shore, a few empty beer cans and broken bottles were scattered around a fire pit, used not so long past. She thought of her father and the Naatucks, only two nights past, discussing her around the fire. And what were they saying now? Was her father worried? Did he care?

She slowed. Perhaps the shed housed a skunk, a badger, or even a bear.

"Hello in there!" she called, just to alert any critter that might be taking shelter. She didn't need any more surprises, thank you very much. With the toe of her sandal, she eased the door open. Dim light traveled through a tiny clouded window. She listened, but it was quiet, so she set Sentry down on the dirt floor. This time, he hopped toward a corner, as if to help her explore the shed's contents.

As if checking out a child's play area, Alex surveyed the floor for anything that might be dangerous. Lures, gasoline spills, stuff like that. A rusted anvil, a few shriveled spiders, not much that looked risky. And no sign of bat droppings.

Next she turned her attention to something for fishing. She found a bucket, rusted bottomless. A few old woodworking tools that she couldn't name. A rumpled magazine, which she glanced through—"Good grief!"—and tossed back on the shelf. Nothing useful. Then she spotted, under an inch of dead flies and dust on the tiny windowsill, a single rusted hook attached to a small ball of fishing line. She picked it up and painstakingly untangled it, no more than the length of her arm. How could she catch anything with so short a line? Still, it was better than nothing.

Sentry tilted his head toward her, as if waiting for her, trusting her to provide for him.

"You're going to stay here while I fish," she said. "Wish me luck." Before leaving him alone, she spotted a small wooden bowl that lay upside down on the floor. She picked it up and a gray spider darted from beneath it. Alex flinched, but she didn't scream. She hustled outside, dipped the bowl in the lake, and returned. "Here," she said. "Water. But you're going to have to drink it on your own."

Sentry opened his beak, as if in protest. Maybe eaglets this age wouldn't drink from a dish; they probably got their liquid from what their parents delivered to the nest. She'd just have to hope, and if the bowl was still full later, she'd have to help him.

First she needed bait. Without a minnow net, she couldn't catch minnows for bait. She'd use worms. With one last glance, she scanned the shed for a shovel. No such luck. Then she closed the door and stepped back into the sunshine with her hook and hopelessly short line.

Without a shovel, she'd have to dig with her hands or a rock. Worms liked to burrow deep in rich, black dirt. At her grandparents' cabin near Brainerd, the cabin she'd visited every summer until she was nine, she had always found worms in the dirt-filled wooden box in the backyard. It had been Alex's job to find the worms and put them in a can. It had been her father's job to put them on the hook.

Behind the shed she found a flat, sharp-edged rock the size of a Grandma's Pantry pancake and headed with it toward a patch of ferns. Sandy soil wouldn't do. She'd have to get into a shady, tree-filled area where there would be dirt. She surprised herself suddenly. She was a Californian, now, not a north-woods girl. But she knew more than she realized.

She stabbed her makeshift spade into the ground and hit rock more times than not. Finally she plumbed a patch of soft earth where a tree had rotted and found several earthworms wriggling in the exposed dirt. She grabbed them—one, two, three, four—then darted back to the cabin, grabbed the chipped coffee mug off the table, and dropped her worms in it. At the soil patch, she grabbed a handful of dirt, added it to the cup, and headed to the dock. She felt a little like Tom Sawyer, goin' fishin'. She tried to think of heroines, girls who had survived in the wild. She thought of the girl in *Julie of the Wolves* and the one in *Island of the Blue Dolphins*. Other than those—her mind drew a blank.

"Okay, then," she said. "How about Alex Castille-Reed?" She spotted a freshly chewed branch onshore that must have floated across the channel from the beaver's work. It was about five feet long. Perfect for a fishing pole. Alex grabbed it, stripped it of its remaining branches, and tied the fishing line on its narrowest end, just above a knot in the wood to keep the line from slipping off. Then she headed to the end of the dock. "Come one, come all!" she called. "See the mighty fisherwoman!"

Her words echoed off the shores.

Opposite her, the beaver kept chewing, as if he'd seen people here before. That was hopeful. Maybe the cans and broken bottles meant it was a party place and somebody would be here sometime before the snow fell.

She sat, fingering a worm out of the mug, its brown body marked by a thin mauve belt. Even a worm could be beautiful, if you looked at it closely. She tried not to think about it, about what she had to do. Sentry was waiting for food, food his parents were not going to deliver. She had to catch a fish. But—as flight attendants reminded passengers before takeoff—in the event of an emergency, a parent is supposed to secure her own oxygen mask and *then* that of her child. If Alex passed out from hunger, she wouldn't be any use to Sentry at all. So she'd feed herself first, as selfish as it seemed.

With quick determination, she pushed the sharp hook into the worm and threaded it onto the hook, piercing it two more times.

If she had a bobber on her line, she'd know when she had a bite. She'd simply have to concentrate, and if a fish hit, she couldn't be lost in thought. Her dad never did understand her daydreaming. Sometimes she would be humming a song, watching the clouds, or thinking about school. One time, she'd been sitting in the grass next to the front yard sidewalk, studying ants travel in a single-file line to and from their tiny sand mound. Suddenly her dad was standing beside her. "Alex, I've been calling and calling.

You haven't heard me?" She hadn't. Her mind did wander, but that didn't mean daydreaming was bad. It just wasn't his way, that's all.

Suddenly she caught herself doing just that. Sitting cross-legged and *daydreaming*. The poor worm was dangling above the water at the end of her pole, drying out in the sun, when it should be in the water as fish bait. Alex shook her head. Maybe there were times when it was perfectly okay to daydream, and then there were times when you had to discipline your mind to stay focused. Like right now.

She held the stick, her fancy fishing rod, and dipped her line into the lake. The worm sank and rested less than two feet from the surface. Tiny ripples traveled out in rings from where the worm had landed. Water beetles no bigger than ladybugs swirled past the line. Her only hope was that a fish would swim by and show some interest.

Alex glanced up, looking for adult eagles in the perfectly blue sky. She didn't really expect to see them, but she wished they would come looking for their lost eaglet. They would know how to feed it, how to keep it alive. The sky was big and empty.

The top of her head, her nose, her arms and legs grew hot in the sun's rays. She eyed some shady spots near shore, but with such a short line, fish would have to be nearly beached to get to the bait. That wouldn't work. The end of the dock was better. She wished she had inherited her mother's bronze skin, like Abuela Elena, who had moved to California from Mexico City eons ago. Though Alex wasn't as fair skinned as her father, she had a tendency to burn, like him. She usually lathered herself in sunscreen for protection, but now she'd just have to sit on the end of the dock and sizzle like a sausage on a grill.

Of course, a little sunburn was the least of her worries. She kept her eyes on the line and the water beyond. Don't daydream, she told herself. Hold perfectly still. She didn't want to scare any fish away, or worse yet, not be ready to give the line an upward jerk when she felt a solid tug. "You have to set the hook," she remembered her dad saying. She *had* paid attention. There were lots of things she remembered.

Like the day they'd gone canoeing on the reservoir outside San Jose. The sun was high, like now, and the water reflected the trees and greenery around the water. Just her dad, mom, herself, and Jonathan. Mom had packed a backpack of sandwiches, nectarine juice, and granola bars. "It's nice here," her father had said, paddling the canoe at the stern, "but it's just not Minnesota." She remembered her parents had guarded their words with each other. They floated along, Alex and Jonathan in the middle. "Alex," her mom said, "your dad and Jonathan have to go to Minnesota for a while."

"But . . . not us?" Alex had asked. They had always taken family trips together.

"Jonathan needs to see some doctors at the Mayo Clinic."

Jonathan—head down, purple life jacket, bare legs extended—rolled a yellow Hot Wheels car up and down the curved walls of the canoe. He didn't have a care in the world.

"But why not here in California?" Alex asked. She remembered Grandma and Grandpa Reed had always talked about the Mayo Clinic in Rochester, Minnesota, as the "best hospital in the world." But she didn't want her brother to go so far away. "There's plenty of doctors here."

"We want him to see the very best."

"Why, does he have cancer or something?" She couldn't fathom now why she had guessed it—cancer—had even known the word back then. She was in second grade and spent most of the canoe ride threading the tip of her tongue through the wide space from her two missing front teeth. A big deal, back then. But kids know more than adults often think they do. She had gone to her first funeral when she was in first grade. She knew people died from cancer. Grandpa had.

Her mother hadn't answered, just looked over Alex's head at her father. Then she nodded, her brown eyes pooling with tears, and whispered, "Something is growing in his brain—" She had turned around in her seat and run her hand across the top of Jonathan's head, rumpling his hair.

"Something that shouldn't be there—called a tumor—and they need to take a closer look at it."

Alex's throat felt hot, remembering. She had gotten so angry, she had done the very thing her parents had always warned her not to do. She jumped up and stood in the canoe.

"He does *not* have cancer!" she shouted, as if the will of an eight-year-old could hold back the world, as if anyone could stop what was to come. She had, however, managed to get the canoe tipping so badly, wobbling side to side, that in three seconds the whole thing went over.

Only Jonathan came up laughing.

That was the last time they went canoeing together. She pictured her whole family again, flying out of the canoe in every direction, which in some ways was pretty funny, now that she thought about it.

CHAPTER THIRTEEN

To Catch a Fish

Alex watched her line. Shadows danced beneath the surface. A school of minnows swarmed past, then disappeared under the dock. With food like that in abundance, what fish was going to want her measly worm?

Her legs were numb from sitting so long; as she moved them, a zillion tiny arrows shot through her feet and ankles. Her eyes were sore from the sun's glare on the water. Nothing had happened for at least an hour. But if she gave up too soon, Sentry wouldn't survive. He wasn't old enough to fish on his own yet.

She worked her side of the channel while the beaver worked his. Occasionally she moved her line a little more to the left, then a little more to the right. But she hadn't gotten as much as a bite.

She stood, stretched, and walked to the shed to peek in on Sentry. He was perched on the anvil, a few inches from the ground. Not exactly an eagle's aerie. Then she returned to her post and changed the worm, now dead and unappealing, for a fresher, wigglier one. Focus, she reminded herself again. Concentrate on the line.

The beaver continued munching green leaves and chomping down saplings. He'd swim down the channel, then return again. Perhaps he had a family somewhere. A beaver lodge with little beavers scampering about. Or maybe he was alone, like her.

As the sun's rays turned to shadows in the channel, Alex identified more and more with the guy in that story her teacher had read to the class: "To Build a Fire," by Jack London. Alex had enjoyed the story, listening with her head on folded arms at her desk, her teacher's words painting a frosty world, so different from the crisply warm autumn air in San Jose. Lost in the woods, the man begins to freeze. Strikes matches futilely. Can't start a fire. And then, when you think he must get rescued, his last match goes out and you know he doesn't make it. Ms. Ramous explained that the author had written two different versions of the story, one where the guy makes it, one where he doesn't. The well-known version is the story where he doesn't. It made no sense not to write a happy ending. But then, she had to admit, the story had haunted her, stayed with her far longer because the main character had died. Died because of his own arrogance. His own *hubris*, that was the word her teacher used. "An inflated sense of pride in one's own abilities." That character needed no one. *Thought* he needed no one.

The end of the stick bent slightly toward the water. The line pulled taut and the tip of her fishing pole arced. Alex held tight and rose to her knees. She didn't know quite what to do. She couldn't exactly reel it in. Her stomach fluttered. She'd actually . . . caught . . . a fish.

She really needed this fish, *couldn't* let it get away, and gave her makeshift fishing pole a tug, hoping to set the hook. Hunched over, she walked her short line alongside the dock toward shore, gently tugging the line, not allowing it to go slack and give the fish a chance to escape. Then, just as the fish began to thrash at the surface, she flung it clear out of the water onto the shore, stick and line still attached.

Plop!

Thrashing and flopping in the grass was a northern. She recognized it by its long, skinny body, its mouth of razor teeth. It was smaller than many of the skeletons they'd found at the base of nesting trees. The more it flopped, the more tangled it became in the line and the more its slime picked up dirt and flecks of leaves, as if coating itself to be batter fried. Maybe she should just wait until it flopped itself to death. But that would be cruel. She had to put it out of its misery.

"Stay there," she said, ran to the shed, and grabbed the rock she'd used for digging. Only two nights earlier, she had watched Ned club the head of a fish to get it to stop thrashing. She had hated watching him, vowed she would never do that. But here she was.

"I'm really sorry," she apologized, "but I have to do this."

Using the flat of the rock, she gave the fish a quick pound between its eyes. It stopped moving. For a few moments, she watched it, expecting it to twitch. Its underbelly was silvery-white, its scales a mix of greenish-blue, gold, and olive. Its eye began to gloss over to a milky white. Gingerly she opened its mouth and pulled the hook free from its jaw. One fish would help ease her hunger, but the hook might determine whether she survived. She placed it on the top of a stone, then surveyed her catch.

Grilled fish. She could almost taste it. Her stomach panged at the thought. She'd build a fire, feed herself first, then the eaglet. If she had caught one fish, she could certainly catch another. And if she had to, she'd catch a snake. One of her father's books showed an eagle eating a snake. Garter snakes could be added to Sentry's menu—in an emergency.

She left the fish on the ground and strode purposefully into the cabin. Matches, that's what she needed. She found an empty book of matches on the mantel. She tossed it aside, worthless. She crossed her arms, scanned the room, the windowsills. Nothing. On the dusty mantel she noticed a metal device, a half-foot long. She picked it up. Like a scissors, she worked the handles. The device clicked. She squeezed the handles together again. This time a spark snapped at the pointed end of the device. It was a fire starter of some sort. Yes!

She ran with it out the door, set it by the fire pit, then gathered loose sheets of birch bark and twigs from around the cabin. She made a small A-frame structure for her fire: two logs in a tepee, one crosswise, and then she built up the birch bark and finer twigs against the crosspiece so that air could circulate around the first flames, just as her father had taught her. Before she tried lighting it, she needed more wood on hand.

The fish was still on the ground, dead as could be. Alex scanned the trees, hoping the bear wouldn't return. If it did, she'd chase it away. Never had a fish been so valuable.

She had to hurry. Next she made a wider arc around the cabin, stooping over and picking up anything that looked burnable. All the logs she found were soaked from rain, far too wet to burn. She kept searching. Finally a foot-wide crawl space at the back side of the cabin caught her eye. It was a perfect space for a den or an ideal spot for a cabin owner to store supplies. She got on her knees and peered in. Dusty air tickled her nose. Alex pushed her body in a little farther. Her hands were on dry dirt. She gave her eyes a moment to adjust to the darkness and found before her a stack of shingles and next to that a small pile of boards.

A distant drone grew louder. Not a boat this time. Something else.

Alex scrambled out from under the cabin just as a yellow float plane flew the over the island.

"Yes!" Alex shouted, fist raised. She jumped to her feet and made her way to the dock. No sense in missing her ride, this time. She waved, but the plane veered sharply south, its tail turned toward her as it droned away.

"Hey!" Alex screamed, jumping up and down. "Come back! Come back! Come baaack!" A lost person only got so many rescue attempts. Arms limp at her sides, she just stared. Her words bounced back, mocking her.

CHAPTER FOURTEEN

Venturing Farther

Alex yanked out eight discarded dock boards from under the cabin. They were rotted, but dry and burnable, and she stacked them by the fire pit.

Squatting before the kindling, she squeezed the metal igniter. *Click, click,* nothing. *Click, click, click, spark!* She pointed its nose against a curl of birch bark. Twenty tries later, a spark licked the bark and a small flame lit.

"I did it!" she called, as the flame sputtered out and died.

"Noooooo." Again Alex worked the igniter, clicking away until her hands grew sore. A spark flickered, lit, and this time the flame traveled from one piece of bark to the twigs she had so carefully lined up. "If I had a saw," she said, glancing at the boards, "I'd cut them up." But she didn't, so she carefully crisscrossed four boards over her small A-frame fire and hoped they would catch. Slowly, gradually, the fire grew and held. Alex found a nearby sapling, yanked off a long branch, and turned it into a roasting stick. She washed the fish in the lake, then pierced it through from mouth to tail and held it over the flames. Its scales turned black from smoke and fire.

When the fish began to fall from the stick, she knew it was cooked. She dropped her dinner onto a fairly flat fire-pit rock—her dinner plate—and began to pick the skin away with her fingers. The fish was cooked just right. Not translucent, but firm and white. It flaked beneath her fingers. She savored every mouthful, careful not to swallow bones. Never had she eaten anything so good. Guilt panged her, knowing that Sentry was still waiting. She ate quickly.

As soon as she finished, she grabbed the skeleton and head and tossed it in the shed for Sentry. "An appetizer," she said.

Then, stomach full and satisfied, Alex returned with a fresh worm to the end of the dock. She was an expert now.

Deerflies began to descend on her head, burrowing one by one into her scalp. She pinched them beneath her fingers and tossed them aside. Nothing was going to stop her from catching another fish. By late afternoon, as she began to think about catching snakes, she got a bite. Her line tugged beneath her grip, and she gave her fishing pole a jerk to set the hook. This time, she pulled a walleye clear out of the water. It flew from her hook, hit shore, and began to flop its way toward water. Alex caught it in both hands, knocked it out with her hammering stone, and headed to the shed.

Sentry was in the corner, wings out. He lifted his head, tongue fluttering rapidly, beak wide. Still, he didn't rise to his legs.

"Hey, I brought you a real meal," she said, fish in her hands. She set the small walleye, maybe a pound or two at most, in front of the eaglet.

Sentry wobbled to his legs, his broken wing hanging awkwardly. For a moment, he paused, cocking his head sideways, eyeing Alex.

She sat down on the shed floor, cross-legged, just three feet away, and watched.

The eaglet hopped to the fish, stood on it, sinking his talons into his meal. With his beak, he pulled at the scaly flesh and swallowed, the food bulging at times in his throat before traveling to his belly.

"I prefer it cooked," Alex said, "batter fried, or grilled with a bit of lemon or cilantro."

Her mother was wild for cooking with cilantro. She grew a pot of it in the small bay window in the kitchen and cut a few leaves for nearly every meal. By now, her father would have called to tell her mom she was missing. Wouldn't he? Maybe he and her mom didn't have much in common anymore, but he certainly would let her know that their daughter had disappeared. He would have returned with the Naatucks to find a canoe gone and Alex missing. They would piece it together quickly. She had taken out the canoe and the storm came up, catching her off guard and setting her adrift. She hoped her dad would keep searching for her. A pang of guilt hit her. She certainly hadn't acted glad to see him. And it wasn't that she didn't want to see him. Deep down, she wanted more from him, more than he knew how to give her. By now, maybe he'd had enough of her.

Sentry worked at the walleye with amazing precision, using his viselike talons to grip the fish and his sharp beak to shred flesh from bone. He didn't stop eating until the fish was whittled down to its bony spine. Then he looked at Alex, as if to ask, "More?"

Alex smiled. One fish made all the difference. The eaglet was looking brighter eyed.

"Now you're probably going to want a nap, huh?" She remembered the downy-lined eagles' nest. The dirt floor of the shed wasn't much of a nest in comparison. She headed to the cabin, grabbed the wool shirt, and took it back to Sentry. "Here," she said, patting the large jacket into something like a nest. He eyed it suspiciously.

"Don't complain yet; I'm not done." She hiked toward

the creek, remembering that she'd seen a patch of grasses near shore. Gathering an armful, she returned to the shed, dropped the soft long grasses onto the wool fabric, and made an indentation, perfect for nesting.

"That's the best I can do," she said with a shrug. "Take it or leave it."

She closed the door firmly, added two more boards to the fire in case a plane flew by, then walked to the island's western point in hopes of flagging down an approaching boat. She gazed out. To the southwest, a boat traveled along the lake, impossibly far away.

Closer to her set of islands, a colony of seagulls colored a small rock island white with their wings and droppings. A few gulls lifted to the air, hovered on the current, then dropped to their rock island again. Seagulls, her father had explained, mate for life. They may separate and fly south with different flocks, but when they return north in the spring, flocking up by the thousands, waiting for the ice to go out, they find one another, recognize each other's cries. Alex couldn't help thinking that somewhere along the way, her parents must have stopped recognizing each other's cries. Maybe the same had happened with herself and her dad.

The sun hung down, three-fourths of the way across the sky. Its rays were hot, warming the rock slabs beneath her. Alex inhaled deeply. The air was sweet with pine, earth, and plants in bloom. And fish. She studied her hands, dark with dirt and fish slime. Sweat glued her hair to the back of her neck. The water looked so good, so inviting. And if she'd earned a moment to relax, this was it.

She pulled off her sandals, her jeans, her tank top. She held out her arms and the sun warmed her skin. Never had she felt so free, so much herself. She was completely alone. Scared, yes. Worried, yes. But something else was seeping into the cracks she would have once called loneliness. She should be lonely. But she wasn't. It was as if she was seeing herself, truly being with herself for the first time.

Water glistened and waves rocked gently against the point. The lake stretched to the western horizon, peppered here and there with islands. She had to be miles from the Naatucks' cabin, with its refrigerator filled with food, Butterball curled on her chair, and her sleeping bag waiting on the porch couch. She would love to be found and back there before nightfall.

For a few moments, she stared. She knew she should come up with a plan, but her mind was blank. The sun nearly sizzled on her skin. The rock was too hot, she suddenly realized, beneath her bare feet.

She stepped closer to the edge of the lake. Waves lapped against the granite ledge that dropped away to a dark, immeasurable depth. Alex couldn't resist. She filled her lungs with a deep breath, pointed her arms over her head, and dove in.

Skinny Dipping

The water felt absolutely delicious against her skin. Alex opened her mouth and drank. Maya claimed that in the middle of the lake, where Alex's island was, the water was safer for drinking. Never completely safe, but safer than shallow bays, where beaver and loon droppings are more concentrated. She was thirstier than she'd ever been, and she filled her stomach with water.

Satisfied, she bobbed in the gentle waves, chilled suddenly by the cool temperatures. If she was going to stay in longer than a few minutes, she'd have to move. She could swim to the other island, check it out.

The crawl was just too much work. She chose a

modified breaststroke, with her head above water so she could see where she was going. In minutes, she covered the distance from Kidney Bean Island to Pencil Island. Her body warmed up from swimming. When she reached Pencil Island's point, she rounded it and swam along its southern shore. Unlike her island, this one dropped off steeply on both sides, like a tall ocean liner. She kept swimming and reminded herself there were no sharks, no manta rays, no jellyfish. Still, she remembered an old photo of a fish caught long ago in the lake, a sturgeon as long as the man was tall. Maybe she was the bait, trolling along in the lake. She kept swimming, her muscles beginning to pinch slightly between her shoulder blades.

Along a sheer rocky bluff, near the waterline, reddish-brown streaks marked the rock face. She swam closer, treading water. She hoped to see pictographs, ancient paintings on rock. Instead, orange lichen covered the rock surface. Her father had told her there were paintings on nearby Lake Kabetogama and that the paintings were likely created by the Laurel Indians, who had lived hundreds and hundreds of years earlier. Somehow those people, and later, the Ojibwe, had known how to live off the land, to survive not only summer but also winter.

And above the people, always, were eagles.

Circling, tending their nests, watching.

Strong, steady creatures. Symbols of wisdom.

She thought of Sentry. Even as an eaglet, he seemed

wiser than she could explain. His whole being radiated an inner strength, a knowing, a sense of being completely centered.

She tried to imagine telling her friends about Sentry, about Rainy Lake. "I was stranded with an eaglet on this really cool island," she might say. Sky-Li would want to hear all about it. "Tell me everything," she'd say, "from start to finish." Mercedes, on the other hand, would listen two seconds, glance at her watch, and say, "I have to run. I'm helping grade papers for Mr. Tienne for bonus points." But trying to put this place into words would be difficult. It wasn't just miles away from San Jose; it was worlds away.

Cupping her hands, she reached forward through the water and pulled back along her sides, propelling herself forward. Halfway along the island's length, she felt winded, but she kept going. She had no choice now.

Choices. Her mom said, "Choose good friends, make good choices." From a distance, her mom had concluded that Alex had gotten in trouble because of her choice of new friends. That was only part of it. The biggest part was her own decisions.

"Stop, Alex," Christina had said the night of the party. She grabbed a green bottle of crème de menthe away from Alex. "What are you doing?"

Alex had grabbed the bottle back and took another sip that burned hot in her throat and warmed her belly. She could barely see the video they'd been watching in Janelle's basement. The drinking had been easy. A fully stocked bar. With Janelle's parents—both stockbrokers—gone until 2 or 3 A.M., Janelle had said, "Go ahead. Sample whatever you want." And so Alex had. A little of this and that. But she knew she didn't want to just taste alcohol. She wanted it to work like the morphine Jonathan had received for his pain, dripping through a tube—*drip, drip, drip*—into the needle strapped on with medical bandages to his thin little arm.

That's all she could think of. After a few sips of something orange, then something red, then something minty green . . . he was all she thought about. At one point, with a purple stir stick, she mixed four or five different sweet drinks together. And the more she sipped, the sadder she became. Clearly not the life of the party. It was as if all the tears she'd held back since the funeral, mostly to please her father, even though he'd never forbid her to cry, churned in her with the alcohol.

"What's wrong?" Sky-Li asked, arm around Alex's shoulders. Even though Alex's mom was concerned that Sky-Li had a pierced tongue and a tattoo—a tiny golden dragon on her shoulder—she was always the first to ask how someone was doing, the one who seemed especially alert to when someone else was hurting.

"What's the matter, Alex? You seem so sad."

Alex shook her head, trying to steady herself on the leather stool.

Music played from the stereo system.

Janelle lit a cigarette behind the bar counter. "My mom's," she said, inhaling and exhaling expertly. "She keeps cartons in the pantry," she added, drawing a puff. "She'll never miss a pack or two." Then she blew smoke out through her mouth and inhaled the curling smoke into her nose. Alex was certain her old friends—friendships formed mostly in elementary classes and in orchestra—weren't smoking and drinking.

"Want one?" Janelle asked, holding the pack toward her.

Alex shook her head. She wasn't going to smoke. That was one path she didn't want to get started down.

Someone suggested going for a swim. "Except Alex," Janelle added. "She can barely sit on that stool!" And the room filled with laughter. Then they were gone, up the stairs, and out the front door.

Alex blinked hard, trying to see. She slid off the chair to wobbly legs but forced herself to follow her friends up the stairs. She didn't want to be left behind, left with her depressing thoughts. She needed to have fun—that's what she was supposed to be doing. Carefully, clinging to the banister, she climbed the stairs and hobbled out the back door. She fell into the bushes—"Whoops!"—laughed to herself, and turned the corner around the house to the swimming pool. Her friends were gone. Underwater lights glowed, beckoning her to the turquoise blue. The last she remembered clearly, her world began to spin and turn black. Minutes later, a neighbor noticed her floating. Someone did mouth-to-mouth, called 911, and an ambulance came and took her to the emergency room. Alex remembered none of that.

Lots of fun.

A real good time.

A loon surfaced near her, its red eye bright against its body of black-and-white feathers.

"Hi, there," Alex said, breathing hard, kicking her legs like a frog.

Then another loon bobbed up, and Alex laughed. "You guys are everywhere." Loons, she knew, mated for life, too. She had to admit, she wished her parents could get back together, had always wished for that. But then, she'd wished Jonathan would have gotten better, too. That was when she stopped praying for anything too specific. She asked for guidance from time to time, but more often it made sense to accept what *was*, what life offered you, at least those things that couldn't be changed.

Right now, the loons were a gift. She watched them from the corner of her eye, just floating along, as if they hadn't a care in the world, and then she swam on.

On Pencil Island's eastern point sat an old car, nearly rusted into the ground. Weeds and a birch tree grew from its skeleton. It looked so strange, so completely out of place. Someone must have driven it, years ago, across the frozen lake and never got it turned around again. It had sat through endless seasons, losing a bit of itself every moment through rain and sun and snow, becoming part of the earth again.

She kept swimming, stroking harder now, trying to counter the chill that crept into her bones on the shadowed side of the island. She swam through the channel, where the water was considerably warmer, rounded the bend, and spotted the painted turtle, sunning itself in a patch of sunlight on the end of the dock. It lifted its head but didn't budge.

The soft hum of a boat passed in the distance, somewhere. Not close enough to matter or to help. Alex swam back to the sandy cove on her island. When her feet hit bottom, she stood, water dripping from her hair and down her skin. She felt good. Alive.

Carefully she picked her path along the island toward the western point. The sun had descended toward the horizon. Perhaps two or three hours left until it set. She still had time to figure out a plan. Until then, she would sun herself on the rocky point before slipping back into her clothes. She lay down and let the rock's heat dry her body. Its warmth seeped into her skin, easing away the knot between her shoulders.

Something wriggled on her ankle. She sat up.

"Oh—gross!" A shiny black leech, about four inches long, clung to her ankle with its round, suction-cup mouth. It must have attached itself while she was swimming. She grabbed its chubby, slippery body and pulled. It stretched like licorice taffy. She groaned, gave it a hard yank, and the leech came free. She flung it into the lake, where it pulsed away, inches below the surface.

Alex examined her ankle. Where the leech had been, blood ran. Leeches injected something—she couldn't remember the name—that made blood flow freely. Alex scooted to the water, rinsed off her ankle, then pressed her thumb hard against the spot for a few minutes to stop the bleeding.

She waited and watched the lake. A boat, as tiny as a crumb, skimmed the lake toward the north. This rocky stretch of reefs and islands probably kept most boaters away, unless they were carefully following a map. She hadn't picked a heavily trafficked island to get stranded on.

She pulled on her clothes and sandals, stood, and headed back to check on Sentry. Her swim had refreshed her, and she felt proud that she'd actually managed to feed herself and Sentry as well. In the growing shadows, she stirred up a small army of mosquitoes from the shelter of leaves and ferns. They buzzed her head, circling, assessing their prey.

She approached the shed. In the damp earth near the door, large padded prints remained. The wooden door was raked with deep claw marks. A nearby branch held a tuft of black fur. Alex glanced nervously around. The bear had returned. She'd forgotten to burn the fish skeletons from inside the shed, to destroy the smell. She studied the leafy shadows around the cabin and in the surrounding woods. The bear must have heard her coming and darted away, just as she neared. Was it watching her now? She had become too relaxed. She couldn't afford to let down her guard again. A few more seconds and the bear could easily have ripped off the door completely. Had he found nothing more than fish skeletons, he might have turned to the eaglet for a quick snack. And as young as Sentry was, he would have flattened himself to the ground, thinking he was keeping himself safe. But he was vulnerable and easy prey.

She opened the door. "Sentry?" she whispered, her earlier confidence now washed out from beneath her.

CHAPTER SIXTEEN

Night Falling Fast

As expected, Sentry had flattened himself in the base of the makeshift nest. "Good," she said, relieved. "At least you're okay." She squatted next to him and placed her hand on his back. Suddenly tired, she wished she could just stay with the eaglet and sleep, but she knew she couldn't. If the bear returned, she would be of no use inside the shed when the door came off. She'd have to stoke the fire, get it blazing, and keep guard.

First she grabbed the bony fish carcasses, tossed them on the fire pit, and closed the door to the shed. Then she gathered more birch bark, built a large mound on the fire's remaining embers, and added the rest of the old dock boards. As she squatted beside the fire pit, waiting for the pile to ignite, mosquitoes buzzed and landed on her neck, her wrist, and her upper lip.

"Good grief!" she said, swatting them away.

Beyond the sand beach and treetops, the sun had slipped from view, leaving a graying amber light. Night was coming. She had to come up with a plan for the dark hours ahead. Even if she got a fire going, the mosquitoes would probably carry her away. The cabin would provide shelter for herself and for Sentry, but she couldn't imagine sleeping in that bat-and-mouse infested hovel.

Her predicament settled heavily on her shoulders. She still hadn't been found. The fire lit and began to burn, sending a thin line of smoke skyward. A seagull flew above the channel, cried once, then flew on again.

Now she had to get serious about getting rescued. She sat cross-legged in the grass and stared into the fire. A spider scurried over the top of a fire pit stone, then disappeared along the stone's white vein of quartz. Flames danced along the edges of the dry boards, the only dry wood on the rest of the rain-saturated island. One day of sunshine hadn't dried out the woods. Her fire might last an hour, two at most.

When her brother had first gone through chemotherapy and lost his rumpled, sandy hair, Alex had asked her father, "Why do they call eagles bald eagles if they're not really bald?"

Her father suggested that when explorers had first seen eagles, they had thought they looked bald because of their white-feathered heads. Of course, they never lost their head feathers and didn't turn white headed until they were four or five years old.

For months, the talk had been nothing but "chemo" and "pain management" and "the best doctors" and "side effects." And Jonathan was gone for MRIs, CAT scans, and blood work more than he was home. For a year, things were hopeful, but then the tumor returned, and this time, he came home to stay. "Inoperable" was the new word, and "Let's enjoy the time we have together." But her parents pulled farther apart, not closer together, and Alex remembered spending hours with Jonathan in the playhouse, with her mom or dad looking in, visiting for tea, but usually one at a time, never together.

Jonathan's hair grew back as fast as his body seemed to shrink. His skin grew pale and splotchy, and he spent more and more time under the quilt. "Tell me a story," he would say, and Alex sometimes sat beside the cot and read slowly from *Charlotte's Web*, and sometimes she just climbed under the quilt beside him and told him about a boy, sort of like him. "He was sick, but much more sick than you, Jonathan, and one day, he stretched his arms—and you know what?"

"What?" he whispered.

"He found out he had wings, just like a bald eagle, and he could fly high above the clouds—"

"Alex?"

"What?"

"Can I have some tea?"

Alex climbed from under the quilt, poured orange juice from the plastic teapot into a teacup, and brought it to her brother. She lifted it to his lips and he drank. Then she wiped his chin with the edge of the quilt and climbed back under the quilt with him, even though it was a warm, summer morning.

"I'm cold," he said, pulling the quilt over his head.

Alex patted his shoulder. "Y'know what?" she continued.

He didn't answer, but she continued, anyway.

"He had eagle vision, like Dad says, and he could see everything from far, far away. No matter how far away he flew, he could always see his mom and dad, and especially his big sister. And one day he decided to fly to Mars, and—"

She stopped. Usually her story went on to trips to Mars, special search-and-rescue missions on Earth, but that day, her brother was so still.

"Jonathan—you sleeping?" She gently pulled the quilt from his head. His eyes were closed, as if he were asleep, but his face—bony as an old man's—was frozen, with just the hint of a smile on his lips. His chest didn't rise or fall. He wasn't making that soft, rushing noise through his nose.

"Jonathan?" she asked again. She laid her head on his chest, against his silent heart, and wrapped her arm across his thin body. The ache in her was bigger than the ocean, and the only thing that could make it worse would be to leave her brother. So she didn't. She rested beside him until his body grew stiff and her father poked his head inside the playhouse door. "Alex?" he asked. "Jonathan?"

"It's your fault," she blurted. "You should have come sooner." But what she believed, what she told herself, was different from her words. She had believed it was her fault. Somehow she still believed it, even though it didn't make sense. If only she hadn't given him the drink, hadn't let him pull the quilt over his head, hadn't let him fall asleep. Maybe they could have rushed him back to the hospital; maybe he could have lived at least a little longer.

And as she remembered, her throat tightened. She missed her little brother. And she knew now why she'd climbed to the eagles' nest to remove the lure. She had needed to help, to do what she could. In part, too, she'd climbed to prove herself to her father, but now everything was different. She needed to protect Sentry and do everything possible to make sure he survived. And she needed to prove herself to herself.

She rose to her feet, wiped her nose with the back of her hand, and opened up the shed door. "Just checking on you, making sure you're still alive."

Sentry glanced up from his nest, following her with his

black eye. He ruffled his feathers, as much as he could with one wing hanging awkwardly over the edge of his new bed. Alex caught sight of her stubbed and blood-crusted right big toe, protruding from her leather sandal, her jeans, torn at the left knee. She didn't want to think about all the bites, welts, and bruises she'd acquired.

"Hey—you and I," she said, sounding more confident than she felt, "guess we're survivors, huh?"

CHAPTER SEVENTEEN

To Build a Fire

The eaglet stood, then wobbled and dropped back down. Alex studied him more closely. His feathers were dull and shabby as an old coat. His broken wing was ragged and dirty. Between his back and head, tiny feathers parted, revealing a scrawny neck. And he was trembling, as if the air were freezing.

"Sentry, you're not feeling well, are you?" she whispered. "Your wing, it needs tending." She didn't know if she should somehow attempt to bandage his wing to his body or leave it alone. He tilted his head, never taking his eye from her. As long as he survived, she could deal with being lost.

129

"You've gotta hang in there," she said. "Please. I'll catch you another fish. Just don't . . ."

She avoided the word and glanced out the shed door. Layers of rosy pink, orange, and amber—like layers of sherbet—filled the western sky. Early evening was settling into night. Sentry wasn't doing so well, and if she didn't start thinking fast. . . . How long could he survive? Food and water might not be enough for him. His wing was busted and that was something she couldn't fix.

"Stay alive," she said to the bird, almost as an order, then gently closed the door.

She grabbed her dirt-stained shirt from a stump, pulled it on, and buttoned it to her chin to protect herself as best she could from bugs. Then she hustled to the end of the dock, sat down, and began to fish again. She'd catch more fish and keep Sentry fed. She watched the line, but she kept glancing at the fire and toward shore, hoping the bear wouldn't return.

Mosquitoes landed on her hands, her neck, her face, and she swatted with one hand and held the rod with the other. Focus on fishing, that was what really mattered. Focus, just focus. She fixed her eyes on the worm beneath the surface, willing a fish to come her way.

Instead of a fish, a memory surfaced, came to her, against her will. The night after Jonathan's funeral, when everyone but her grandparents had left her family to return to their own lives, Alex had woken up in the middle of the night with a start. The sound of a siren filled her room, filled her head. Sirens weren't uncommon, but this one was so close, shrill and demanding. She had glanced out her upstairs window at lights that flashed red. And at the corner of her backyard, a pillar of orange flames and black smoke rose to the sky. The playhouse was on fire!

Alex dashed into the hallway. "Mom! Dad! Fire!"

"What? Where, honey?" In the darkened hallway, Abuela Elena put her arm around Alex's shoulders and hustled her downstairs. At the back door, they stared out.

Silhouetted by the flames, in the midst of a half dozen neon-clad firefighters, her father stood, back to them, watching the playhouse burn. Off to the right, her robed mother spoke with a police officer. Alex rushed out from Abuela Elena's firm squeeze, barefooted on the grass, and wrapped her arms around her father's waist. "What happened?" she cried, her voice filled with tears. Her tea set, her grandma's quilt, books she had read to Jonathan, and so much more were lost to her now. She felt an urge to run to the inferno and rescue what she could, but she knew better. Losing her brother was the worst thing she could have ever imagined, but strangely, seeing the playhouse in flames cut her more deeply. "Dad? What happened?"

For a few moments, her father didn't answer. "Too many memories," he said, his voice distant and above her. "I couldn't bear to look at it anymore."

His words slid off her, but then slowly, to her horror, she grasped their meaning. "Dad . . . you mean, you . . ."

He rested his palm between her shoulder blades, limp and heavy. He didn't answer, his silence sealing his guilt. He just stared as the firefighters hosed the flames back until the smoke finally cleared. Alex pushed away from him then, ran to her mother's side, and stared at the black skeletal remains of the playhouse.

From that moment, it was as if he'd swept her brother from her life. And she couldn't forgive him for it.

Her father had burned the playhouse out of desperation. She knew this now. He had acted wildly from a pain so deep that for a moment it had made him crazy. Still, he might have thought about her feelings.

She glanced over her shoulder at the cabin. She couldn't go on pretending she would be rescued any moment. Sure, someday someone would come to the island, but that might not happen soon enough to matter. The eaglet wasn't going to last without getting help.

In the waning light, a sparrow flitted from above the cabin toward the lake, right over her head. One sparrow, then another.

She looked again. Not sparrows. She hunched into her shoulders. Bats. A third bat, its wings black wisps, darted past.

Alex flinched, then ducked, and remembered that bats

move by sonar. She didn't have to worry. They wouldn't fly into her. She studied the air. A column of bats rose like smoke from the cabin's chimney and fanned out into the evening air to begin their hunt.

Her chest filled with a sense of doom that she couldn't shake. It was Sentry, the way he was failing. The bats, the waning light of day, the slipping into night. She began to breathe hard, fast, and her heart accelerated. She couldn't do this. She couldn't last forever on this island. Couldn't face another night.

A crazy, desperate idea formed in her mind.

She dropped her fishing pole on the dock, rose, and walked to her fire, still burning bright. She grabbed the unburned end of a stick, lifted it from the fire, and walked through weeds to the cabin. She carried the burning stick up the steps and pushed open the door. It was a good little cabin—a cabin that had sheltered her for a night. Someone had loved it once.

Alex swallowed hard, her throat suddenly sandpaper dry, and walked across the uneven floor. The stick smoked and its flame died, but its tip glowed red. Who knew how long ago someone had left this place or why? Shirts and jackets hung on wall pegs. Boots still waited on the floor. In the gray light, it was almost easy to think their owner would be returning soon. Her nose itched. Years and years of dust and bat dung. No one was returning. Still, she was reluctant. She hated to take this step, but she didn't know what else to do. She had to take the risk.

"I'm sorry," she said, arms beginning to tremble like loose sails in a wind. Hesitant, Alex held the smoldering board before her as darkness slid slowly into the corners of the cabin.

Finally she placed the glowing stick on the bed, then dashed out to gather more birch bark. She returned, tossing it on the stick's red ember, then leaned closer and blew until flames flickered on the birch bark, nibbled at the holes in the blanket, and crept toward the walls, dry as kindling. The insides of the cabin would burn quickly, but the mossy roof would be slower to take hold. With all the recent rain, she hoped the island itself wouldn't burn.

Alex back stepped swiftly to the door, hoping someone would soon spot the fire, a tower of smoke, her desperate cry for help.

Flames licked gingerly, almost reluctantly, at the wooden wall behind the bed, then in a startling flash of light, spikes of fire shot up toward the rafters. Fire billowed and illuminated the room, drawing air in a loud *whoosh* from the open doorway, and the cabin roared to life.

flames

Alex stumbled out coughing, and fell down the steps. She hadn't expected the fire to light so quickly. But the cabin had sat for years, drying to fire-ready tinder, and all it took was one well-placed spark.

Flames reached through the open door and licked at the edges of the moss-and-lichen-covered roof. Hand over her mouth, Alex backed away from the heat and the tower of black smoke. The bats wouldn't be able to return to their rafters at dawn, but they'd find another place to call home.

Next she had to get Sentry and head with him to the island's western point, where they could watch from a safe distance for approaching planes or boats. She entered the shed. "Sentry—" she said, and reached down. Carefully she picked him up, hands against his sides and over his wings, and carried him against her chest. She hoped the giant bonfire would bring help for both of them. But the lake was large, and even if someone in a distant fire tower saw the flames, it would take time before a search boat reached them.

She clamped her lower lip between her teeth and stared, wished she could turn back time and go back to yesterday morning. Go back to when her father had stood beside her bed and asked her if she wanted to join him. All the anger she'd felt toward him suddenly didn't matter.

The fire roared from the cabin door, sending heat from the belly of its furnace. Alex moved away quickly with Sentry until she stood on the sandy shore. This time when a boat came, she swore she'd be ready.

The fire crackled and sent flames and plumes of black smoke into the deepening twilight. Even as she followed the shore toward the point, the blaze spat and roared in the island's cove. Her body filled with adrenaline, and she hurried over boulders, tripping once and landing on her tailbone and elbow, but still she held on to Sentry. "Sorry, fella," she said. She'd feel her fall later, but not now. She had to hurry.

Smoke peppered the air. She hoped she was right about the rain-soaked island. She hoped she hadn't started a fire that would spread beyond the cabin. Certainly that hadn't been her intention. But her father was right. There were times when you had to be decisive, times when emotions were better placed on a back burner.

Sentry struggled in her arms.

"Sentry," she said gently, "I'm not gonna hurt you. I want to help." The eaglet lifted his head slightly, opened his sharp beak, but his movements were weak and unconvincing. He tucked his beak back into his chest feathers again. Alex wanted to cry. She'd really made a mess of things. She hoped, prayed, she could make things right for him—for her.

Her heart drummed in her ears. Smoke plumed. Fire glowed above the treetops. Sentry shuddered and struggled again, but then he settled, his talons relaxing. Alex thought she could almost hold him now like a baby and let him rest in the crook of her arm, but she didn't.

Carefully she made her way along the rest of the shore to the point. She stood on the slab of rock that had earlier warmed her. Now she hoped it would provide a spot where she could be seen. But the sun had set, and only a dim glow, like a flashlight losing power, remained on the horizon.

Then, to her surprise, a boat appeared, swerving around the point of Pencil Island. As the boat slowed its motor and turned in her direction, the glaring white beam of a spotlight crisscrossed the channel and suddenly fell on

Alex, just for a moment, then passed on. The boat turned, and she found herself again in shadows. "Oh, pleeeease," she called.

Just as she filled her lungs to yell, the boat's light swerved back, right on her. It puttered closer and closer, its light blinding Alex, until its bow touched the shore.

Alex blinked, turned her head from the light.

"It's her—we found her!" a girl shouted.

"You're the girl we saw on Skipper Rock the other morning—the one everyone's searching for?" a boy asked, jumping out and pulling the boat closer.

"I knew if we kept looking," the driver said, a boy nearly her age. "The wind was blowing this direction, like I said."

It was the same boatload of teenagers who had warned her away from the eagles' nest only a morning before. It couldn't have been so short a time. Not days. Months, more like.

"Help," Alex managed in a whisper, her breath lost somewhere on the night air. Within moments, several hands eased her and the eaglet into the boat, and she sat on the seat behind the driver.

Alex began to cry, and once the tears started down her face, she couldn't stop. The teenagers began to ask questions, but she was in no shape to answer. She held on tight to Sentry. All her strength slipped down to her toes, and her body sagged from within.

The boat rumbled away from the island, its gas fumes puffing above the motor. Behind them, a glow rose from the island's cove. She prayed that the fire would be contained to the cabin and, if it began to spread, that firefighters would get there soon enough to keep the fire from destroying the whole island. She had only wanted to save the eaglet and herself. Would she face criminal charges now?

Once they had cleared the islands and reef, the driver pushed the throttle forward, and the bow climbed up through the water. They raced westward toward Dryweed Island, passing by several boats and beneath a couple of planes, which were heading toward the flames.

Beneath the hood of her sweatshirt, a girl peered at Alex and shouted above the motor, "What happened?" Alex shook her head. Too much had happened. She just wanted to get back. She would talk, later, if anyone was interested, but not now. She held the eaglet, felt his tiny heart fluttering against her own. Felt the weight of its life against her chest, in her hands. She wished he hadn't fallen and hurt himself. She wished Jonathan hadn't had to suffer, wished he were still alive. From what she was learning about life, it was pretty clear that no one could hold back pain and tragedy forever. All anyone could do was try. Try to do the very best you could in the circumstances that life handed you. And often, despite your best intentions, you made a lot of mistakes along the way.

Her dad had traveled all the way to Rochester with Jonathan, doing the best he could, but it wasn't enough to keep his son alive. And in his deep hurt—a hurt that she had felt, too, a raw pain that had zigzagged through her whole being and made her feel as if she were in someone else's skin—in that kind of hurt, her father had set the playhouse on fire. For the first time, she felt she understood . . . and she forgave him.

Drawing a long, ragged breath, Alex filled her lungs with lake-scented air, then slowly exhaled. She tilted her head back, tasting tears. Stars flickered above, and the Big Dipper tipped its handle in her direction. A wellspring of gratitude filled her, washing over her and through her. She was grateful. That was it. Grateful—maybe for the first time since Jonathan had died—to simply be alive.

She looked back at the island, a dazzling orange jewel against a blanket of navy blue. Blueberry plants, she had been told, grew thick after fires. And someday, where the cabin had stood, trees would grow, pushing up out of the thin soil that covered the island's rocky spine. She hated to have had to set the cabin on fire, but she was relieved beyond words to be carried by the boat to safety.

The island receded in the distance, smaller and smaller, until it became a mere firefly in the night.

CHAPTER NINETEEN

Special Cargo

The Naatucks' cabin was lit up for a party, or so it seemed when the boat pulled toward the dock. White ground lights lit the steps from dock to cabin. Alex had given directions from memory, as best she could, and the speedboat's driver, whose name was Nick, found his way slowly through the darkness, running lights on. From the back of the boat, a pole light glowed, lighting up the faces of her rescuers.

The air temperature had dropped, and she shivered, as much from the cold as from knowing that in moments she would have to face her father, have to explain everything.

The boat coasted in neutral and Nick grabbed the side

of the dock. "This is the place?" he asked, turning to Alex.

Alex nodded.

One of the girls tied a stern rope through a metal dock ring. Just as one of the guys was securing a bowline, lights from another boat curved around the point toward them. The boat came in fast, cut its motor, then drifted to a perfect landing on the opposite side of the dock. Alex glanced over.

Ned was at the wheel, and her father was flying out of the boat, running a hand through his hair, then snapping his cap back on his head.

Nick honked the boat's horn. *Wonk-wonk! Wonk-wonnnnk!*

Alex turned away and hung her head, the eaglet resting against her chest. He was so still now, she wasn't even certain he was alive. She swallowed back tears. She had to get out of the boat; she knew she needed to move. But she sat glued to the seat.

"Got some news?" her father asked from the dock, his voice pressing toward them.

"I think so," Nick said, his forearm curved casually over the steering wheel. He tipped his head in Alex's direction.

"Well?" Her father's voice was impatient, unsteady, as if he'd been holding himself in check. In the dim light, in the cluster of bodies, it must have taken her father a moment to see her.

"Alex?" He jumped into the boat, right in the midst of the teenagers, and crouched on his haunches in front of her. "They found you! I'm so—are you okay?" His words spilled out in an avalanche. This wasn't like her father.

"Let me look at you. I thought we'd lost you—they found the life jacket, then the canoe." His words filled with tears and he barely whispered. "Thought you'd drowned."

Alex forced herself to raise her head, to meet his eyes.

Stubble covered his chin. His eyes were streaked red and shadowed, his face crumpled with emotion. She had never seen him cry before. Not once.

"It needs help, Dad," she managed. "Its wing—it's broken."

Her father looked closer in the soft glow of the boat's stern light. "An eaglet—what in the—where? How?"

"Can we take care of him first, then talk—later?"

With experienced hands, as Alex held its legs, her father felt along the eaglet's body and wings. "How long ago did you find it?" he asked, shifting to his eagle expert voice. Alex felt herself relax, relieved to see her father take charge. She didn't want to be strong anymore, at least not for a little while.

"Yesterday morning," she said. "I tried feeding it."

"At this age and in his condition," her father said, "it might last two, maybe three days at most out of the nest. It needs help—just as soon as possible."

The teenagers waited quietly, listening.

"Your mom flew in this morning," he said. "I called her last night—I was a real mess. I kept thinking, we lost Jonathan—and then possibly you." His breathing was labored. "Alex, I . . . it's so *good* to see you!" He smiled then, leaned over the eaglet, and kissed her forehead. When had he last done that? When would she have allowed him to do that? Not in years.

"C'mon," he said, gently putting his hand on her elbow and helping her from the boat with the eaglet.

"Hey? Maybe we could stop by tomorrow," Nick said, glancing up from beneath his fishing cap, "to hear the whole story?"

Alex nodded.

"I owe you a huge thanks," her dad said, shaking Nick's hand. "To all of you."

When Alex stepped into the cabin—aware she was probably a study in scrapes, welts, and gnarled hair—she was sure she would melt to the floor. But she stood with the eaglet, her father's hand on her shoulder, and her tears fell fresh.

"Look who's—" her father began, voice unsteady.

Alex's mother, with a cry of pain and joy, tossed aside a blanket and jumped from the couch. "Alex!" Hair falling loose from a clip, mascara streaked, she stopped short when she saw Alex's bundle. "I see you're not alone," she said. Then, like a mother examining a newborn, she ran her forefinger alongside Alex's right cheek, then her left, then across the welts and scrapes on the backs of Alex's hands, as if to see for herself that her daughter was real. "Oh, honey," she said, eyes brimming. "I was so worried!"

Maya sat against the arm of the couch and Ned stood beside her; they looked on, as if respecting Alex's parents' need to be close to her.

"How'd those kids find you, Alex?" Ned asked.

"There was a little cabin on the island." She hated to admit what she'd done, but there was no getting around it. She had to tell the truth. "I set it on fire, hoping someone would see it. They were out looking for me. . . ."

"So your plan worked," Maya said, smiling. "Good thinking."

Alex nodded. "Yeah, I guess so." Her arms were heavy. "Can we talk about me later? This eaglet needs help."

She was relieved, at least for a few minutes, *not* to be the center of questions and attention.

Maya found a cardboard box, cut in a set of air holes, and lined it with a Garfield beach towel. Alex gently set Sentry inside, not quite ready to let go, then she sat on the nearby couch, leaned against her mom, and looked on.

Ned came from the kitchen with a handful of microwave-thawed smelt. He tossed the small silvery fish in with Sentry, who immediately started pecking at the food. "I knew those would come in handy sometime," Ned said, winking at Maya.

From the plaid chair, Butterball stirred, arched her back, then lifted her nose in the direction of the box.

"That's right. Eat up, little fella." Ned looked to Alex. "Ready to close it up?"

She nodded, and he eased on the cover. "Bon voyage, little one. Next, shipping tape?"

Maya tossed him a roll of transparent tape.

Arm snug around Alex's waist, her mother turned and asked, "Why not let your dad take him in? You could stay here, you know. Rest. Get cleaned up."

Despite her mother's and Maya's best efforts at getting her to stay, Alex insisted on joining her father. She had to see Sentry on his way. Maya loaded her up with a yogurt drink, a thermos of chicken noodle soup, and crackers. Alex's mother pressed her face against Alex's cheek. "See you real soon," she whispered.

Under a star-stitched sky, loons called wildly back and forth from bay to bay, their songs haunting and beautiful. As Alex and her father boated the short distance to the mainland, Alex held the box steady in her lap.

To Alex's amazement, her mom said she was staying on for a week or so, that she and Dad had talked. That she needed a vacation, anyway. Her father's backpack and sleeping bag were tucked beside the living room couch; in the room where he had been staying, Alex had noticed her mother's black leather bag on the bed.

Alex wouldn't get her hopes up—she knew better than

that—but who was she to argue if her parents wanted to spend time together. After all, they weren't divorced yet.

When they reached the marina, they tied up to the dock, climbed into her dad's Jeep, and headed with Sentry to the small airport terminal outside International Falls. On the ten-mile drive, Alex explained everything to her father. The lure. Her climb. How awful she'd felt when the eaglet fell to the ground. How she'd intended to return, but lost her paddle and had drifted, drifted, drifted.

"It's all right," he said, listening, nodding. "It's all right."

And when her words stopped pouring, he glanced at her. "Y'know, honey, you did a good job of keeping that eaglet and yourself alive. That's what counts, Alexis."

A good job. She soaked in the words. And for once, she didn't mind being called Alexis. "But the fire," she asked, "am I in trouble?"

"Ned said he'll look into it. The Park Service may ask for restitution for firefighter expenses, if necessary, but since you were only trying to get rescued, not vandalizing, I think they'll cut you some slack."

Alex sniffed, her emotions a thin thread from the surface. "I hope," she said.

Northwest Airlines gave special flying privileges to injured raptors, especially eagles, and her father had called ahead to make sure they had space on the day's last flight to Minneapolis. When they arrived, the airport was nearly empty. They didn't have to worry about waiting in line.

The ticket counter agent, her red hair pulled back in a ponytail, taped a label, SPECIAL CARGO, on the box. "We'll take good care of it," she said proudly. "Don't worry about a thing."

"Thanks so much," Alex's dad said. "Someone from The Raptor Center will be there to meet it."

"Him," Alex said, not taking her eyes off the box, now on the floor beside the ticket agent. She worried he wouldn't survive. Could he recover from the trauma she'd put him through?

"Him?" her father asked, turning away with her toward the exit doors. They walked a few paces, then paused, her father's eyes meeting hers.

"It was the smaller of the two eaglets," Alex explained. "I'm sure it's a male. His name is Sentry."

He nodded slowly, a half smile playing on his weathered face. "I see. I could sure use an eagle expert like you, y'know."

She smiled teasingly. "I know."

"I'm serious. If all goes well, I hope to return him, I mean Sentry, to his nest—a lure-free nest now, I might add—before his sibling fledges. That way the parents would care for him until he can fly and find food on his own. But I have a problem—"

"What?"

"That tree on Skipper Rock. Not that I want you climbing to eagle's nests, but just once, I may need someone who's lighter to help me get Sentry back in his nest. One month, if all goes well. That's what they predicted at The Raptor Center. Anyway, want to stay around here till then?" He looked hesitant, like a plane stalling in midair, about to crash.

Alex knew the answer immediately. She wished she could fly along with Sentry all the way to Minneapolis and sit with him during his recovery. But if she could be part of actually returning him to his nest, that would be even better. She nodded. "Count me in."

A smile spread across her dad's face, feathering the creases at the corners of his eyes.

Alex yawned, aware of a deep tiredness, as if she'd been carrying around the enormous weight of a voyageur's pack for years—a weight that had finally lifted. She touched her father's hand.

"Let's go, Dad."

As part of my research for this novel, I joined a small, dedicated team of eagle experts on Rainy Lake for a few days. While the climber scaled the tree and the team waited below, I thought I'd be taking notes and shooting photos from a distance. Instead I found myself near the base of several nesting trees, holding the legs of nearly adult-size eaglets or recording and measuring, as I was instructed. That's one of the things I love the most about writing—I never know where my research will take me next.

Eagle researchers do fieldwork to study how eagles are faring. When eagle populations plummeted in the years following World War II, eagle researchers found that a pesticide, DDT, and related insecticides were being consumed by eagles through the food chain, which resulted in paper-thin eggshells that cracked before eaglets were ready to hatch. The eagle population in the United States, outside of Alaska, dropped from an estimated one hundred thousand bald eagles to an alarming low of 417 nesting pairs. The eagle was classified an endangered species in 1967, and laws were made a few years later that banned the use of DDT. Gradually the eagle population began to recover.

Today—thanks to the help of biologists, researchers, and a more informed public—eagles have made a tremendous comeback. And eagle research continues. Because the eagle is at the top of the food chain, ingesting everything its prey has consumed, it is one of the first creatures to exhibit dangerous levels of heavy metals, pesticides, or other pollutants. As one of the researchers put it, "When the eagle is doing well, the rest of the creatures in that environment are also likely fairing well."

Long considered a spiritual messenger of wisdom by Native Americans and our national symbol for freedom, the bald eagle still fills the skies with its heart-piercing cry. May we be watchful enough to catch a glimpse of an eagle in flight; may we be quiet enough to hear its voice on the wind.

—M.C.

www.raptor.cvm.umn.edu
The Raptor Center, St. Paul, Minnesota.

www.barrharris.org
Barr-Harris Children's Grief Center in Chicago
offers an extensive book list for children and adolescents.

www.hospicenet.org
This comprehensive site includes articles
on talking to children about death and loss.